Quasar Was in Danger!

Max heard a latch rattle, followed by the familiar sound of a stall door sliding open and a horse's feet clopping on the concrete floor.... He saw a person in the dim light, leading a horse....

"Keith," he whispered fiercely ... "Someone's taking a horse out!"

The two boys cautiously peeked over the hay bales, just in time to see Quasar's hindquarters and tail heading out the door....

They climbed over the bales as fast as they could ... and hurried to the edge of the barn door and peered into the darkness.... Max spotted the shape of a person and horse moving down the path toward the woods. "There he goes," Max said, pointing at the thief leading Quasar away. "Come on!"

The two ran down the path after the horse thief. Suddenly, the person turned and stopped.... Max couldn't make out the person's face in the shadows. Whoever it was wore a dark jacket with a hood. Max couldn't even tell what color hair the person had.

The thief tied the lead rope to either side of the horse's halter, then leaped expertly onto Quasar's back. Max realized that the thief would outdistance them in no time on horseback.... Suddenly the rider stopped, turned Quasar, and trotted directly toward the bushes where Max and Keith were hiding.

"Duck!" Keith whispered.

Max ducked his head and held his breath, his heart pounding. He heard Quasar's hoofbeats pass right by them on the path, just a few feet away. As the hoofbeats grew fainter, Max peeked out of the bushes in time to see the rider urge Quasar into a canter, vanishing in the dark woods beyond the path.

Books in the SHORT STIRRUP CLUB™ series (by Allison Estes)

#1 Blue Ribbon Friends
#2 Ghost of Thistle Ridge
#3 The Great Gymkhana Gamble
#4 Winner's Circle
#5 Gold Medal Mystery

Available from MINSTREL BOOKS

Gold Medal Mystery

Allison Estes

A MINSTREL® BOOK

Published by POCKET BOOKS
New York   London   Toronto   Sydney   Tokyo   Singapore

This book is a work of fiction. Names, characters, places and incidents are products of the author's imagination or are used fictitiously. Any resemblance to actual events or locales or persons, living or dead, is entirely coincidental.

A MINSTREL PAPERBACK *Original*

 A Minstrel Book published by
POCKET BOOKS, a division of Simon & Schuster Inc.
1230 Avenue of the Americas, New York, NY 10020

ISBN: 0-671-00099-3

First Minstrel Books printing October 1996

10 9 8 7 6 5 4 3 2 1

SHORT STIRRUP CLUB is a trademark of Simon & Schuster Inc.

A MINSTREL BOOK and colophon are registered trademarks of Simon & Schuster Inc.

Front cover photo by Pat Hill Studio

Printed in the U.S.A.

*For Beth Darlin' and Jimbo
at the real Thistle Ridge Farm,
with love and thanks.*

"Short Stirrup" is a division in horse shows, open to riders age twelve and younger. Additional requirements may vary from show to show.

Gold Medal
Mystery

1

MAX MORRISON AND HIS BEST FRIEND, KEITH HILL, trotted their horses bareback across the back pasture of Thistle Ridge Farm. A high hill crowned by one giant sycamore tree loomed before them. Max glanced at his friend, a smile beginning to spread over his face.

"Race you to the top," Max said.

"You're history," Keith replied.

At the same moment, both boys dug their heels into their horses' sides and leaned forward as they cantered toward the hillside together. Both horses were copper-colored chestnuts with white faces. They were exactly the same height: about fifteen hands at the withers. Their white-stockinged legs flashed through the grass as they cantered up the hill, perfectly in stride. The two horses seemed identical, except Max's gelding, Popsicle, had blue eyes.

"Yee-hah!" Keith yelled, trying to get his mare, Penny, to pass Popsicle. Penny snorted disdainfully at her young rider. *You must be kidding,* she seemed to be saying, as she simply refused to leave Popsicle's side.

As they approached the top of the hill, Max was laughing out loud. "That's the trouble with trying to race Popsicle and Penny," he panted as Popsicle reached the crest of the hill and walked.

"Yeah. They like each other so much neither one will pass the other," Keith complained, as Penny walked along beside Popsicle. "We'll never find out who's faster because every time we race it's always a tie!"

The horses ambled into the shade of the big, old sycamore and immediately began to graze. Like their horses, the two boys were exactly the same size, though Max was eleven and Keith was ten. Each boy wore cut-off shorts, a green T-shirt, and scuffed, brown paddock boots. And they each wore a bright nylon cover over their safety helmets. But under his helmet, Keith's face was dark tan, with sparkling brown eyes and shiny, longish black hair. Max had lighter skin and hair and blue-gray eyes.

Max wiped the perspiration from under his eyes, enjoying the breeze that blew across the ridge, stirring the leaves of the old sycamore. He admired the smooth, spotted bark of the old tree, letting his gaze drift upward until he glimpsed the blue summer sky through the leaves of the topmost branches. He let one hand slide back, patting his horse gently, before he leaned slowly all the way back and laid his head on Popsicle's rump. The horse didn't seem to mind having a boy lying on his back instead of sitting up. Popsicle just kept grazing contentedly.

"Ahhh." Max sighed, keeping one hand on the end of the reins as his other arm and legs dangled around Popsicle's sides. He closed his eyes, testing his balance as he felt his horse take a step forward. Popsicle's hindquarters lifted and dropped as he walked, searching for a fresh clump of grass. Max's head bobbed along with the horse's movements. It was such a funny sensation, he couldn't help laughing.

"Max, look," Keith said.

Max sat up and looked across the pasture where Keith was pointing. He could just make out two riders trotting across a stretch of bottomland. One was on a black pony and one was on a dapple-gray. Max recognized his twin sister, Megan, on the gray pony. The other rider was Megan's best friend, twelve-year-old Chloe Goodman.

"It's Megan and Chloe," Max said, watching the two girls. "I wonder if they're looking for us."

"Let's ambush them," Keith said with a gleam in his eye.

Max saw that he and Keith could go down the other side of the hill, circle around, and sneak up behind the girls. It would be fun to scare them. "Okay, come on," he said, picking up the reins.

The boys headed down the hill and trotted around the base of it to a little creek shaded by trees that ran along one edge of the pasture. They found a place

3

where the sides of the creek weren't too steep. Max and Keith leaned back as the horses picked their way carefully down the bank and waded through the shallow water. Then the boys leaned forward and grabbed mane, holding on tightly as the horses scrambled up the other side. Max had expected to see Megan and Chloe just ahead of them, but the girls were nowhere in sight.

"That's weird," Max muttered, scanning the rolling hills and wide, flat stretches of land that sprawled all around him. "They should have been right here, but they're nowhere in sight."

"Where could they have gone?" Keith said, sounding puzzled.

Just then, Popsicle's and Penny's heads shot up. Both horses and boys were startled by the thudding of hooves and two loud whoops right behind them. Max turned around, his heart thumping, as Megan and Chloe trotted up beside the boys.

"Gotcha!" Megan yelled gleefully.

"Were you surprised?" Chloe asked hopefully.

"No way," Keith said.

"Yeah, right," Megan joked. "Then how come you almost fell out of your saddle just now?"

"Megan!" Max yelled. "Are you trying to kill us? You're not supposed to come trotting up on other riders like that. You could have spooked Popsicle and Penny!" He was lecturing his sister about safety, but really he was just annoyed that the girls had managed to sneak up on them.

"Well, we didn't spook the horses, did we?" Megan

4

said. "Besides, you were going to do the same thing to us, weren't you?"

Max scowled. It was true; he and Keith would have done the same thing, so he really couldn't be angry. "How'd you find us?" he asked.

"Oh, you guys think you're so cool," Megan teased. "Chloe and I have been following you all morning, haven't we, Chloe?"

"Yep." Chloe nodded her head. "We followed you all the way from the tree that was struck by lightning."

"We followed you around the lake and through the pine woods," Megan taunted. "We knew where you were the whole time."

"And you never even saw us." Chloe giggled.

"Aw, man!" Keith exclaimed.

"You guys want to play hide-and-seek?" Megan asked.

"Nah," Max said. "Let's ride through the creek. It's so low now, I bet we can follow it all the way back to the barn." The creek that bordered the south end of the pasture was sometimes waist-deep in places. But in the midsummer heat, it had shrunk to a shallow trickle. Max turned Popsicle back toward the creek, saying, "I saw a cowboy movie where the bad guys tried to escape in a river, but the sheriff and his posse tracked them, even through the water."

"Cool!" Keith said, following along on Penny. "We can be the outlaws."

"Nah, let's be the posse. The bad guys always end up getting caught," Max said.

"Hey, wait for us!" Megan called. She and Chloe

followed the boys back down the bank and into the creek.

"Shh," Max told them. "You can't make a sound, or we might miss an important clue." He bent low over Popsicle's neck to duck under an overhanging branch. Popsicle stopped and began to splash at the water with one front leg. Still hunched over, Max tried to urge him forward. He squeezed Popsicle firmly with both of his legs, but Popsicle didn't budge.

"You'd better kick him, Max," he heard his sister warn.

Popsicle splashed bigger and harder and began nodding his head vigorously up and down, as if he were telling himself what a great idea it was to play in the water. Max still couldn't sit up; he was stuck under the tree branch. "Uh-oh," he said as he felt Popsicle's front end drop toward the water. Max began to cluck frantically at Popsicle, thumping the horse's sides with his heels.

"He's going to lie down!" Keith yelled. "Watch out, Max!"

But it was too late. Popsicle plopped down in the shallow creek and rolled over on his side. Max had just enough time to hop off, but he still ended up sitting in the creek. He stood up slowly, his shorts dripping. There was nothing to do but hang on to the reins and wait for Popsicle to finish rolling.

"Max, are you okay?" Chloe asked anxiously.

"I'm fine," Max said quickly. He was a little embarrassed but unhurt.

"I never saw Popsicle do anything like that," Megan said, laughing.

"I guess he wanted a bath," Max observed.

"Or he wanted *you* to have one," Megan joked.

All four kids laughed. Popsicle just kept on lying in the creek. He seemed to be enjoying the cool water.

"Come on, Popsicle." Max clucked at his horse. "Get up, now." He tugged a little on the reins and said hopefully, "Please?"

Popsicle seemed to be deciding whether or not to get up, but finally he did. Then he gave a great big shake, splattering water all over the place.

"Hey, watch it!" Keith put an arm up to shield his face.

The girls squealed and tried to back away. Popsicle was spraying everyone.

Max began to laugh. "I guess he thought everybody needed a shower."

"Let's get out of here," Megan said. "I think I've had enough of this creek."

Max managed to climb back on his horse's slippery back. Then the kids rode along the creek until they found a spot where the bank was low enough for the horses to climb out again. The four riders ambled through the pasture, talking and laughing together.

"I can't believe we're actually going to the Olympics!" Max said for the hundredth time.

"I know!" Keith said. "It's going to be so cool."

"I can't wait to see Sharon ride," Chloe said.

"Me, too," Megan said excitedly. "I hope she wins a gold medal on Quasar!"

Sharon Wyndham, the owner of Thistle Ridge Farm, was a member of the United States Equestrian Team. She had competed in the equestrian events at the Olympic Games twice before, on her two big Dutch warmblood horses: Cuckabur, her jumper, and Quasar, her dressage horse. This year, Sharon and Quasar had qualified for the Three-Day Event team. She had already shipped Quasar to the International Horse Park just outside Atlanta, Georgia, to begin the final preparations for the Olympic games.

Sharon was also Max and Megan's trainer. Max remembered how he'd hated moving from the town in Connecticut where he'd lived all his life to Hickoryville, Tennessee. But now he was glad his family had moved. A lot of good things had happened to him since he came to Thistle Ridge Farm. He'd met Keith, and the two boys had become best friends. He was taking riding lessons from an actual Olympic rider. And now he had tickets to the Olympic Games!

Max, Megan, Keith, and Chloe, otherwise known as the Short Stirrup Club, had won the tickets in a team competition earlier in the summer. The four kids had formed the Short Stirrup Club when Megan and Max had first come to Thistle Ridge Farm, right before a big horse show. It had been Chloe's first show, and she'd been really worried about it. She didn't have any show clothes and was scared that Bo Peep would buck her off right in front of the judge. Worst of all, she had to ride against snobby Amanda Sloane on her fancy pony, Jump For Joy. Megan, Max and Keith had managed to teach Chloe to sit a buck. They'd even scrounged up proper show clothes for her. Best of all, they'd persuaded the Sloanes to give Jump For Joy to Chloe when he injured his leg in the horse show.

Since then, Max, Megan, Chloe, and Keith had become the best of friends. As the Short Stirrup Club, they had had several adventures, some scary and some funny. And now they were going to the Olympics! Max could hardly believe it. He had always dreamed of going to the Olympics, but he never imagined he'd actually get there. In three more days, though, he'd be heading for Atlanta, where the games were being held. He could hardly wait!

James Morrison, Max and Megan's dad, would drive the kids there. James Morrison was a famous artist. He'd been selected to paint scenes of the equestrian games at the Olympics.

Like his father, Max was talented at drawing. But it was Megan who really took after her dad. She had her father's sturdy build and the same thick, wavy brown hair and brown eyes. In fact, Megan and Max were so different that their mother was always saying she didn't know why they bothered to be twins. Rose Morrison, the twins' mother, was head of the orthopedics unit at the brand-new medical center twenty miles away in Memphis.

Max was proud of his parents, but they were very busy. His mom worked long hours at the hospital. Sometimes she even spent the whole night there, if she had to do emergency surgery. Max's dad painted portraits of famous people, which meant that he was always traveling. Max missed his father a lot when he was away. Lately, he had begun to wish that his dad had a regular kind of job like other fathers, who went to work in the morning and came home at the same time every night. Max was looking forward to spending a whole week at the equestrian games with his dad.

The horses and riders were almost within sight of the barn, when Max heard a dog barking. He looked across the pasture and saw a small black-and-white shape bounding toward them through the stubbly grass. "Look, it's Merlin," Max said.

"What's he doing way out here?" Keith wondered.

Merlin was the friendly border collie who lived at Thistle Ridge. He belonged to Jake Wyndham, Sharon's husband. Merlin had the run of the whole farm, but he could usually be found at Jake's heels. In no time, he had reached the group of children on horseback.

"Hi, Merlin," Max said. "C'mere, boy." Max whistled and patted his thigh. Merlin trotted over to him, and Max bent down to pat Merlin's head. Then the dog did a curious thing. He circled around behind the four riders and crouched low. Next he charged at Popsicle, who was at the edge of the group. Popsicle gave a snort and quickly trotted forward toward his friend, Penny.

"Hey!" Max cried, startled at the dog's behavior.

"What's he doing?" Megan said.

Bo Peep was in the back of the group now. Merlin

crept toward her with his belly close to the ground, then sprung at her, nipping the air. The fat black pony kicked up her heels in annoyance. Chloe was tossed forward onto Bo Peep's wide neck, but she managed to grab mane and cling with her legs to keep from falling off.

All the horses were trotting now. They held their heads high and swung them from side to side, looking for the dog. Merlin kept moving back and forth in a semicircle behind them. If one of the horses moved away from the herd, he'd charge at that horse, nipping at its hocks until it moved back to the group.

Max shortened his reins and sat up tall. He was glad that Popsicle's trot was smooth; it made it easier to stay on. But he didn't understand why Merlin was behaving so strangely. "Do you think something's wrong with Merlin?" Max asked.

"Maybe he has rabies or something," Megan said anxiously.

"Oh, no, do you really think so?" Chloe asked, sounding scared.

The horses kept trying to head toward the barn, but Merlin was moving them across the pasture toward the woods near one of the paddocks. Suddenly, Max realized what Merlin was doing.

"You guys," Max said. "Merlin's a shepherd's dog. He's *herding* us!"

"But why?" Keith said.

"And where?" Megan said.

Through the trees, Max glimpsed the tailgate of

Jake Wyndham's blue Ford pickup truck. Thistle Ridge Farm was nearly a hundred seventy acres of wood and pastureland. Jake drove all over the farm in his truck, repairing the fences, checking on the cows he kept in one of the pastures, or just looking after the place. On a farm that size, there was always something that needed tending to.

As they came around the edge of the trees, Max was in the lead. Merlin's barking became more urgent, and he left the group of horses and ran around to the front of the truck. Then he ran back to Max and barked loudly at him.

"What's the matter, Merlin?" Max said to the dog. "Jake?" he called, looking around.

"I don't see him," Keith said. "That's funny. I wonder where he is."

Max walked Popsicle around the side of the truck, where Merlin had gone again. Then he saw why the dog was so agitated, and he felt his stomach do a flop.

"You guys, it's Jake!" Max called. "I think he's hurt!"

Jake lay on the ground near the front of the pickup truck. His eyes were half open. He seemed to be trying to talk but could only mutter something Max couldn't understand. Merlin licked frantically at his master's face. Jake moaned and closed his eyes.

"Jake!" Keith yelled. He jumped off Penny, leaving the reins hanging down to ground-tie her, and ran to Jake's side. "What's wrong with him?" he asked Max.

Max saw the fright in his friend's face. For a second, Max couldn't think what to do. Jake seemed to be getting worse. His face had turned from healthy tan to ashen gray. He trembled and moaned again.

Max didn't know what was wrong with Jake, but he could tell that he needed medical attention. "Stay here with him!" Max told the other kids as he turned Popsicle around. "I'm going for help!" He picked up a canter and started for the stables.

2

MAX WAS A CAUTIOUS RIDER WHO NEVER WENT TOO FAST, and Popsicle was a calm, laid-back horse. But Max knew this was no time to be laid back. Popsicle was cantering slowly around the back paddock fence. Max urgently thumped the horse with his heels and clucked, pushing the reins forward. Popsicle broke into a gallop. Max didn't think twice about how fast he was going. He didn't even remember that he was riding bareback. He wasn't frightened for himself at all. He just knew he had to help Jake.

Max leaned forward to stay with the rhythm of the gallop. Popsicle seemed to feel how urgent it was that they get to the barn. Max saw a determined look in Popsicle's eye as the horse dug hard into the earth with each stride. The wind streamed past Max's face, and his thigh muscles began to burn with the effort of holding himself on the horse's smooth back.

Finally they were in sight of the barn. Popsicle put on another burst of speed and they flew the last fifty yards up the hill to the pasture gate. For a moment, Max considered jumping over the gate. They were only a few strides away. The gate seemed to grow higher as they approached it. *Can we do it?* Max wondered. He knew Megan had jumped it accidentally once on her pony, Pixie. Max made up his mind. "Come on, boy. Let's jump it," Max said to his horse. He bent forward and grabbed mane, closing his eyes and clenching his teeth as he waited to feel Popsicle launch himself over the four-foot gate.

A second later, Max was glad he had grabbed hold of the mane—it saved him from getting thrown over his horse's head as Popsicle came to a sliding stop just inches from the gate. The horse stood patiently, waiting for the gate to open. Max was off his back and through the gate in a second. He didn't bother to close the gate but ran as fast as he could into the barn, calling for help.

Horses snorted with surprise as Max raced down the barn aisle leading Popsicle, who trotted behind him willingly. The horse's shoes seemed to ring out an alarm as they clopped urgently on the concrete floor.

"Hey!" Max shouted. "Allie, somebody, anybody!"

Usually, the barn was busy with grooms brushing horses and mucking out stalls, and boarders fussing over their horses. But for some reason, the barn seemed empty of people. The only sound was of horses busily munching their midday grain. Max realized it must be after noon; the grooms were all at lunch. He tried to think. Where would he find Allie Tatum, the head groom? He ran toward the office and pounded on the screen door.

With an annoyed look on her face, Allie stuck her head out of the office. "What in the world are you beating on the door like that for?" she said. She held a sandwich in one hand, but when she saw Max's face, she nearly dropped it. "What's wrong?" she said, her tone instantly changing to one of concern.

Max was gasping for breath from all the riding and running he'd just done. Before he could answer, Pepper Jordan, the veterinarian, called out a friendly greeting from the front door of the barn. Max turned to face him. When the doctor saw the panicked look in Max's eyes, he hurried toward him. "What's the matter, son?" he asked.

Max took a gulp of air and managed to speak. "Dr. Pepper," he said, "it's Jake! Something's wrong with him!"

"Where is he?" the vet demanded.

"At the edge of the woods, down by the back paddock," Max told him. "Hurry, Dr. Pepper," Max pleaded. "He doesn't look good!" For the first time since he'd found Jake, Max thought he might start to cry.

"Come on, son, show me where," Dr. Pepper barked. He started for his truck, calling back over his shoulder, "Allie, call nine-one-one! When the ambulance gets here, send them straight down to the back paddock!"

Max handed Popsicle's reins to Allie and dashed after Dr. Pepper. The vet started up the truck and slammed it into gear. Max was thrown back against the seat as the truck lurched forward. They headed through the open gate and down the hill, the truck jouncing crazily on the uneven ground. Max gripped the door handle hard to keep from getting bounced around. He had just enough time to describe to Dr. Pepper how he'd found Jake before they caught sight of the blue pickup.

In another second, Dr. Pepper's truck roared around the trees. Max braced himself as they screeched to a halt. He saw Chloe and Megan holding Penny and the ponies. Keith knelt beside Jake, a frightened expression on his face. Dr. Pepper nearly tore the door handle off getting out. He sprinted to Jake's side, with Max right behind him.

"Oh, Dr. Pepper, what's wrong with him?" Keith asked. "He's been making terrible sounds, and sort of shaking. And look, he has some kind of cut here. It's bleeding." Keith's eyes were full of tears as he pointed to Jake's lower leg. Blood trickled from two holes in the worn denim of his jeans.

Dr. Pepper didn't speak. He checked to be sure Jake was breathing, then ripped open his bag and took out a stethoscope. For a few tense seconds, he listened to Jake's heart. Then he pulled Jake's eyelids up, checking his pupils. Jake shook his head slowly from side to side, mumbling something.

"Jake," Dr. Pepper said. "Jake, can you hear me?" He peered anxiously into his friend's face.

Jake struggled to open his eyes. For a second, he seemed to recognize the vet. "Cottonmouth," he managed to say. Then he couldn't hold his eyes open anymore.

"Max!" Dr. Pepper called. "In the back of my truck, in the refrigerator, there's a blue metal box. Bring it here, quick!"

Max ran to the back of the truck and tugged open the heavy camper door. He found the box and brought it to the vet. Dr. Pepper was rummaging through his bag. "Open the box," he directed Max.

Max's fingers trembled as he fumbled with the latch, but then he managed to open it. The box was filled with little boxes and bottles of medicine. Dr. Pepper ran his fingers lightly over them, searching for the right one. When he found it, he tapped it. "That one. Take it out," he told Max as he flipped the cap off a syringe.

Max pulled the bottle out of its box. "Antivenin," he read as he handed the bottle to the vet. Then Max guessed what had happened. "Did a snake bite him?" he asked.

Dr. Pepper nodded as he expertly filled the syringe and gave Jake an injection. "A cottonmouth moccasin," Dr. Pepper said. "There aren't very many poisonous snakes around here, but a cottonmouth's sure one of them. Must've been a big one, too, by the look of that bite." He indicated the wound on Jake's leg with a nod of his head.

"Will he be all right?" Keith asked worriedly.

"He will now," Dr. Pepper said. "You kids did a fine job. If you hadn't gotten help right away, it'd be a different story." He smiled reassuringly at Keith and the other kids before he began to examine the snakebite.

Max heard the faint wail of a siren drifting down from the highway. In a few more minutes, the emergency vehicle pulled up. The paramedics had Jake in their truck and on the way to the hospital in no time. As he watched the truck drive up the hill, Max felt relieved. Dr. Pepper had said that Jake should be just fine.

"Max," Keith said, "you were awesome."

"I never saw anybody gallop so fast bareback," Chloe said. "I would have fallen off if I went that fast."

"Way to go, Little Brother," Megan said with admiration.

Megan was twenty minutes older than her twin, and she loved to remind him of it. Max usually came back with a name for Megan when she called him "little brother," but this time he didn't mind. A warm feeling began to fill his stomach and crept up to his heart. Max felt good. More than that, he felt proud that he and Popsicle had been able to do something to help Jake.

"I guess the Short Stirrup Club really saved someone this time," Max said. He grinned at his sister and his friends and stuck out his hand. Keith stepped forward and laid his hand on top of Max's. The girls led the ponies up to them, and added their hands to the pile.

"Short Stirrup Club!" they cheered together.

Suddenly, Max remembered who had really saved Jake. "Merlin!" he said. He looked around for the dog and spotted him sitting forlornly near Jake's truck. "Here, Merlin," Max called. He whistled softly, the same way he'd heard Jake whistle for his dog. Merlin's ears pricked up at the sound. He got up and trotted over to Max, wagging his tail. "You're a good boy, Merlin," Max said, stroking the dog's soft ears.

"He sure is smart," Keith agreed.

"It's a good thing Merlin found us and brought us to Jake," Chloe said. Her green eyes grew wide as she realized what could have happened. "If he hadn't, Jake might not have made it."

For the rest of the afternoon, and all the next day, Merlin stayed at Max's heels. The border collie followed Max all over the stables, even to the bathroom, where he scratched at the door and whined until Max let him in. Max felt sorry for the dog, so he tried to pay special attention to him. He patted him and talked to him and brought him treats to eat.

On his second day without Jake, Merlin wasn't any happier. He seemed lost without his master. When Max's dad came to pick up his children, Merlin followed the Bronco to the end of the driveway, then howled sadly and lay down looking miserable. Max hated to leave him like that. It made him feel like howling, too.

"Gosh, Max," Megan said, "I think Merlin's adopted you."

"He's just lonely, I guess," Max said, watching the dog grow smaller and smaller as the Bronco pulled away. "He misses Jake."

"When will Jake be out of the hospital?" James Morrison asked.

"In a few more days, probably," Max told his father. "Allie said she saw him today and he was looking much better."

"That's good," James Morrison said. "By the way, I want you and Megan to be extremely careful when you're out in the pasture. There's at least one dangerous reptile lurking around out there."

"You mean the snake," Megan said.

"Jake will find it and kill it when he gets better," Max told his dad. But he was still thinking of Merlin. Tomorrow they would be leaving for Atlanta. Max was excited about the trip to the Olympics, but he was a little worried about Merlin. He hoped the dog would be all right without him. He'd begun to feel as if Merlin belonged to him, and Merlin certainly seemed to feel the same way. As soon as Jake came back, Max knew, that would change. But he was sort of enjoying looking after the dog. Max had never had a pet, except for Popsicle. But horses were different. A horse couldn't come home with you, or lick you all over, or sleep in your bed.

"Dad," Max said.

"Max."

"Could I have a dog of my own?" Max asked hopefully. He studied his father's expression in the rear-view mirror.

"Max. We've been through this before. You know I'm allergic to dogs," his father told him.

Max sighed. "I know. But how about if it lived outside? You wouldn't have to feed it, or even go near it. I would take care of it. Please, Dad? Pretty please?"

"If he gets a dog, then I get to have a cat," Megan said.

"Megan!" Max hissed at his sister. He jabbed her with an elbow, and she jabbed him back.

"No cats, either," the twins' father told them. "Besides, you're both busy enough with your horses. How would you have time to care for cats and dogs, too?"

"How about fish, then?" Megan tried.

"Fine. As long as you feed them and clean the tank."

"Goody!" Megan said. "Max, what kind of aquarium should we get, fresh water or salt water?"

But Max just shrugged. He didn't care anything about fish. He wanted a dog. He understood that they couldn't have a dog in the house, because his dad was allergic to them. But he didn't see why they couldn't keep one in the yard. It just didn't seem fair.

Max moped through dinner. Then he and Megan spent the evening packing for the trip to Atlanta. By the time he closed his suitcase, Max wasn't thinking about dogs anymore. His head was full of *grand prix* jumpers sailing over five-foot fences!

3

EARLY THE NEXT MORNING, MAX HELPED HIS DAD LOAD most of their gear on top of the luggage rack. Then they drove to Thistle Ridge Farm, where they had agreed to meet Keith and Chloe. Keith was already there, sitting on top of his suitcase outside the main barn. He waved at Max and stood up as the Bronco pulled up in front of the stables.

"Where's Chloe?" Megan asked Keith.

"Haven't seen her yet," Keith answered.

"How come girls are always the last ones to be ready?" Max complained.

"Oh, be quiet, Max," Megan told him. "Dad and I had to wait for you to eat three bowls of cereal this morning, remember?"

Max got out and opened up the back of the Bronco for Keith, who threw his bag in. Then the two boys went to say good-bye to their horses. Max slid open the door of Popsicle's stall and went inside. Popsicle nudged at Max's chest with his nose, searching for a treat. Max held out the juicy red apple he had brought for the horse, who slurped and munched it noisily while Max scratched the special spot on his withers. "Good-bye, Popsicle," Max said. "I'll see you in a week. And Allie will take good care of you while I'm away. I'll say hello to Quasar for you," he added, closing the door. He glanced at his hand, which was covered with foamy apple-slobber, and wiped it on the seat of his shorts.

"Max, Keith," Megan called. "Chloe's here. Let's go!"

Max and Keith hurried to the Bronco. Chloe had put her things in the back but had forgotten to close the door. Max slammed it quickly, climbed into Bronco, and buckled his seat belt.

"Everybody ready?" James Morrison asked, glancing in the rearview mirror at the three kids in the back seat. Megan was sitting up front, but they had all agreed to take turns.

"Ready!" four excited children chimed.

"Olympics, here we come!" Max said happily. They backed out of the parking spot, headed down the long, tree-lined drive, and turned onto the highway.

The drive from Hickoryville, where they lived, to the Horse Park in Atlanta would take about eight hours. For the first couple of hours, the kids talked excitedly about the Olympics. Megan said when she grew up she was going to ride in the Olympic Games in the *prix des nations:* the biggest, most challenging jumping competition in the world.

Max could picture himself riding in the Olympics, but he was on a big fancy dressage horse. He imagined himself alone in a spotlight. With nearly invisible signals, Max asked his horse to change the leading leg at every stride of the canter. The horse seemed to skip across the huge arena as they performed perfect *tempe* changes. Once, Sharon had let Max walk Quasar around, to cool him down after a workout. Max remembered how thrilled he had been to be sitting on a world-class dressage horse. Sometimes when he was riding Popsicle, he imagined how exciting it would feel to be on the United States Equestrian Team, traveling all over the world to compete with the best riders of all nations. Max thought Sharon was the most outstanding rider he had ever seen. He hoped that one day he would become as good a rider as Sharon. Maybe he really would ride in the Olympics someday.

Chloe, who was always reading, had brought along a book about the Olympics. She read some of the interesting parts out loud to them as they cruised along.

"It says here that the first Olympics was held in Athens, Greece, in 1896. But they didn't have show jumping in the Olympics until 1912. And most of the riders who competed were in the military," Chloe told them.

"Who won the first gold medal for jumping?" Megan wanted to know.

"A French officer, Jean Cariou, riding a horse called Mignon," Chloe answered.

"Of *course* it was a *man*," Keith kidded the girls.

"Hey!" Megan protested. "Chloe, who was the first woman rider to win a gold medal?"

Chloe studied the book. "Well, it says here that women weren't even allowed to compete in the Olympics until 1956."

"No way!" Megan exclaimed.

"But that year a woman named Pat Smythe led the British jumping team to win the bronze medal," Chloe read. "And since then there have been plenty of great women riders."

"Like Sharon," Keith offered.

"She's the best," Max agreed.

Chloe turned a few more pages in the book. "Listen to this, y'all," Chloe said. "This is the Olympic Oath. It says here that one athlete from the country hosting the Olympics is chosen to take the oath for all the other athletes."

She cleared her throat and read: " 'In the name of all competitors, I promise that we shall take part in these Olympic Games, respecting and abiding by the rules which govern them, in the true spirit of sportsmanship for the glory of sport and the honor of our teams.' "

"That's a good oath," Max said. "Especially the part about the spirit of sportsmanship."

"That's the heart of the Olympic competition," James Morrison said. "Or any goal you set out to achieve. Winning is not as important as the hard work you put in trying to be the best you can be."

Chloe read, " 'The most important thing in the

Olympic Games is not to win but to take part, just as the most important thing in life is not the triumph, but the struggle. The essential thing is not to have conquered, but to have fought well.' That's from the Olympic Creed," she told them.

"Maybe we should make up an oath for the Short Stirrup Club," Max suggested.

"Yeah!" Keith said.

"Great idea, Max," Megan said.

"ACHOO!" James Morrison sneezed for the third time in the last twenty minutes. "I hope I'm not coming down with a cold," he remarked.

For the next few hours, the kids played all the car-riding games they could remember. When they couldn't think of any more games to play, they made up one. It was called "Guess That Horse."

"Is it a stallion?" Max asked.

"Yep," Megan nodded.

"Is it a Thistle Ridge horse?" Chloe asked.

"Nope."

"Is it a famous horse?" Keith asked.

"Yep," Megan said.

"Cuckabur," Keith guessed.

"Nope."

"Give us a clue," Chloe said.

"Okay. It's a racehorse," Megan told them.

"Is he still alive?" Max asked.

Megan shook her head.

"Is it Winning Colors?" Keith asked.

"Keith, Winning Colors was a filly," Chloe reminded him. "And anyway, she's still alive. Now she's a brood

27

mare." Chloe knew more details about all the different kinds of horses and riding than anybody Max had ever seen. He guessed it was because she was always reading books about horses.

"Oh, right," Keith said.

"Is it Alydar?" Chloe asked Megan.

"Nope," Megan said.

"Give us one more clue," Max said.

"Okay, one more, but then you have to guess," Megan said. "He won every race in his whole career, except for one. Now can you guess?"

"Secretariat!" Max and his dad yelled at the same time.

"You got it," Megan told them.

"Did you know that when Secretariat died, they did an autopsy on him? And they found out that his heart was about *three times* the normal size," Keith said dramatically. "My sister told me. They said his heart was just *huge,* and that's probably why he could keep on winning races the way he did."

"It makes sense that a person's or an animal's heart could make them a hero, doesn't it?" Max said.

They played "Guess That Horse" for another hour, but by then the monotony of the long car trip had set in. "Dad, how many more miles is it?" Megan said in a pretend whiny voice.

The other kids instantly joined in on tormenting the twins' dad.

"Are we there yet?" Max whined.

"I'm hungry," Chloe said.

"I'm thirsty," Keith said.

"I have to go to the bathroom!" Max said.

"Ninety-nine bottles of beer on the wall, ninety-nine bottles of BEEEER!" Megan bellowed.

"Oh, no, not the beer bottle song!" James Morrison took both hands off the steering wheel and threw them up in pretend despair. Then he laughed and joined in the song. He sang louder than any of them.

When they had finished the whole song, they were all quiet for a moment. Then Max said, "I really do have to go to the bathroom."

"Me, too," Keith said.

"I really am hungry," Chloe said.

"Me, too," Megan agreed.

"Okay, okay, I get the message," James Morrison said. "We'll look for a place to stop. I need to find a gas station soon, anyway."

They pulled off the highway and found a diner where they could make a rest stop and get something to eat. Then they drove across the street to a gas station. It was a self-service station. Max asked if he could pump the gas, and his dad agreed. Keith got out, and the two boys stood talking while they waited for the tank to fill.

Max remembered that the air conditioning in the Bronco had made him chilly before they stopped. "Hey, Keith, can you get my jacket out of the back?" Max asked.

"Sure." Keith walked around to the back and opened the door.

When the tank was full, Max put the hose away. He was screwing the gas cap back on when he felt a tap on his shoulder. Max closed the little door over the gas tank and turned around.

Keith stood there with a very peculiar expression on his face.

"Did you find my jacket?" Max asked.

"N-no . . ."

"What's the matter?" Max frowned.

James Morrison rolled down the window and said, "What's taking so long there, guys?"

"Um, I can't find your jacket, Max. I think you'd better come back here and find it yourself," Keith said loudly. He motioned Max to the back of the Bronco with a jerk of his head.

Puzzled, Max followed Keith to the rear of the vehicle. His jacket lay on top of the bags, in plain sight. "It's right here," he said, picking it up.

Keith was pointing silently at something. Max looked and at first didn't see anything. Then he gasped. His mouth fell open, and he covered it with his hand.

"Uh-oh," Max said.

"*Big* uh-oh," Keith agreed.

Impossibly squeezed into a little space on top of one bag and between two others was a very familiar furry shape. Two black ears pointed at Max, and a pair of brown eyes peered at him out of a black-and-white face. It was Merlin!

"Merlin!" Max cried in a whisper so his father wouldn't hear. "What are you doing here?"

"What's your dad going to say?" Keith whispered.

"Hurry it up back there, you guys," Max's dad called

to them. "I would like to get to Atlanta before the Olympic Games are over, if you don't mind."

"What'll we do?" Keith asked.

"We won't tell him," Max decided.

"Um, Max, don't you think he's going to find out anyway?" Keith pointed out.

"Not necessarily," Max said. "Merlin's been back here for five hours, and none of us even noticed. Besides, it's not like Dad's going to turn around and drive him back to Hickoryville. He'll just be really mad at us, and maybe make us leave him at the pound or something. We definitely can't tell him," Max said firmly. "At least, not until we get there." Max patted Merlin's head. The dog licked Max's fingers and thumped his tail affectionately in the tiny space he had to wag it in. "Promise you won't say anything, Keith."

"Okay," Keith promised.

"Guys, come *on*." James Morrison's endless patience was wearing out.

"Coming, Dad!" Max called out. To Keith, he said, "Quick, give me your cup."

Keith had been drinking a soda in a paper cup from the restaurant. Max took the cup and poured out the soda, leaving only the ice.

"Hey," Keith protested. "I was going to drink that."

Max set the cup in front of Merlin. "In case he gets thirsty," he explained to Keith.

"Oh." Keith nodded.

They closed the back door and climbed into the Bronco.

31

"What took you so long?" James Morrison asked his son.

"You're always talking about how slow we girls are," Megan remarked.

"I was looking for my jacket," Max explained. "I got cold from the air conditioning."

They pulled away from the gas station and headed toward the interstate. As they picked up speed on the entrance ramp, Keith elbowed Max.

"What?" Max said.

"I just thought of something." Keith whispered in Max's ear. "What if he pees back there?"

Max and Keith looked slowly over their shoulders toward the rear compartment of the Bronco—and saw Merlin's black-and-white head peeking over the top of one of the bags, just inches from Megan's ear. Max quickly tossed his jacket over the dog's head to hide him.

"I thought you needed your jacket," Megan said.

"I got hot," Max explained.

Merlin slowly raised his head again, but this time it was covered with a jacket. Keith reached across Megan's shoulder and pushed Merlin's head down.

"Hey, watch it," Megan said. "You elbowed me right in the ear!" She turned around to see what was behind her. "What are you guys doing back there, anyway?"

Max and Keith exchanged looks. Then Max started to giggle. He couldn't help it. He just couldn't believe that dog had actually sneaked into the Bronco and ridden undetected almost all the way to Atlanta.

"What's so funny?" Megan wanted to know.

Keith was laughing, too, by then.

"Oh, nothing," Max said. He tried to make a serious face, which only made him laugh harder. Soon he and Keith were gasping for breath. Megan gave up trying to find out what the boys thought was so funny. Finally, they calmed down.

For the rest of the trip, Max kept checking to be sure Merlin stayed hidden. Luckily, the last few hours went by quickly, and Merlin made no more appearances. The summer sun was a perfectly round red-orange ball hanging low in the sky as they pulled into the parking lot of the hotel.

"We're finally here!" Max exclaimed.

"Hooray!" Megan shouted.

"Man, will I be glad to get out of this car," Keith said.

"You're not the only one," James Morrison said. He got out and started around to the back.

"Dad!" Max jumped in front of him. "Why don't you go on and check in? We can unload the bags, can't we, guys?" Max said.

"All right," James Morrison agreed. "Be sure you lock up." He headed toward the hotel.

"Phew," Max said when his father had gone. "That was close."

"What do you mean?" Megan asked.

Max opened the back compartment of the Bronco. As soon as he did, a blur of black-and-white fur jumped out.

"Oh!" Megan squealed, startled.

"Merlin!" Chloe said as she recognized the dog. "What's he doing here, Max?"

Max was scratching Merlin's ears. The dog sat at his feet, looking adoringly up at the boy. "I'm not exactly sure," Max said. "We found him back here when we stopped at the gas station."

"Wow, Dad's not going to be too happy about this," Megan said. Then she giggled. "No wonder he's been sneezing all day."

"We're not going to tell Dad," Max said. "Understand?"

"And just how do you plan to keep him hidden, Max?" Megan asked. "They don't allow dogs in hotels."

"We need to come up with a plan," Max said.

"I know!" Megan had an idea, which she explained to the others.

They quickly took the clothes out of Max's large cloth duffel bag and stuffed them into Keith's suitcase. Then Max whistled for Merlin, who was visiting a grassy area near the parking lot. To Max's relief, the dog hadn't peed in the back of the Bronco. Max helped Merlin step into the duffel bag, which was just large enough to hold the dog. He zipped it up, until only the dog's head was sticking out. Merlin seemed to know he'd better cooperate. He sat very still as Max stooped to pull the strap over his shoulder, then stood up, struggling with the weight of the heavy dog.

"Are you okay, Max?" Keith asked.

Max nodded, panting with the effort of carrying the

34

dog. He took little, fast steps, shuffling across the parking lot under his load.

The four children carried all the luggage into the hotel lobby. Max staggered in last. He had pushed Merlin's head all the way into the bag and zipped it closed. He set the bag down for a moment, grateful for the rest.

"We're all checked in," James Morrison said, smiling as he tossed the room key up and caught it.

A bellboy loaded the bags onto a luggage cart. Max held his breath when the fellow picked up the duffel containing Merlin and slung it onto the pile of bags. A muffled yelp came from the bag.

"What in the world was that?" James Morrison asked.

Chloe pretended to cough. "It was me," she lied. "I just got something in my throat." She cleared her throat loudly several times.

James Morrison sneezed again. "Well, I certainly hope you're not getting sick, too," he said to her as they followed the bellboy into the elevator.

As they rode up, the four members of the Short Stirrup Club silently high-fived one another behind James Morrison's back.

"Your plan's working so far," Max whispered to his sister.

"ACHOO!" James Morrison sneezed.

The kids tried their best not to laugh. The elevator doors slid open, and they followed the bellboy to their rooms.

4

MAX WAS CANTERING POPSICLE AROUND A HUGE RIDING arena. His ears rang with the sound of thousands of spectators cheering and clapping for him. He had won the gold medal for his country! As he cantered around he held up the medal; it hung from a striped ribbon and shone softly in the sunlight. The sun was warm on Max's face, too. And wet . . . Wet sunlight?

The roar of the crowd faded as Max slowly realized he was waking from a dream. But the dream was over, and there was still something warm and wet moving over his face. And what was that smell? And why did his chest feel so heavy?

Max opened his eyes. Merlin lay on top of him, fondly licking his face. Max patted his head. Then he remembered that Merlin was supposed to be a secret. He sat up quickly and looked at his father. *Good. He's still asleep*, Max thought, sinking back on to the pillow. He caught Merlin's ears gently in his hands to stop him from licking and peered into the dog's intelligent brown eyes. "What am I supposed to do with you?" he whispered.

Merlin's tail thumped against Max's leg. "Grrruff!" he barked softly in answer.

"Sssh!" Max closed the dog's muzzle with his hand.

"ACHOOO!" James Morrison sneezed loudly.

Merlin barked out loud, startled at the sound. Before Max could grab the dog, he leaped from the boys' bed and landed on top of Max's dad. James Morrison sat up, yelling in surprise.

"Maaax! Why is there a *dog* in my *bed?*" he yelled, sneezing again and again as Merlin licked him joyfully on the face.

Max caught Merlin by the collar and managed to drag him off his father's bed. James Morrison stood up, hands on his hips, and stared fiercely at his son. Merlin barked happily at him.

The girls came out of the small adjoining room where they were sleeping. "Uh-oh," Max heard Chloe say.

"Oopsies," Megan said.

"Busted," Keith said.

Frowning, James Morrison opened his mouth to say something to Max, but *"Achoo!"* was all he managed to get out. He tried to glare at Max again when he had finished sneezing, but his mouth twisted in a peculiar way. Max was surprised and relieved to see his father sit down on the edge of the bed, laughing.

"I should have known," he muttered, shaking his head. "I should have known better than to try to take a work trip with four kids. Okay, let's hear it—how did a border collie get into my hotel room? And while we're at it, is there anything else I should know about? Are you sure I'm not going to discover a kitten in my camera bag? Or a horse in the bathtub?"

The kids giggled, and they promised that there weren't any more wayward animals lurking in the hotel room. Max explained how he and Keith had discovered the stowaway dog when they stopped for gas and how they'd smuggled him into the hotel in Max's duffel bag.

"I should have known," James Morrison said again. "No wonder I kept sneezing in the car. But you should have told me right away, boys, instead of keeping it a secret," he said sternly to Max and Keith.

"Sorry, Dad," Max said sheepishly.

James Morrison sighed. "Perhaps he can stay at the Horse Park while we're here. We'll check with Sharon. And we should call Allie and let her know where he is. Jake would be pretty sad if he got out of the hospital and thought that his dog was lost."

"I didn't think of that," Max said. "Especially since it was really Merlin who saved Jake in the first place. We'd better call right away."

Max's dad called the farm. He spoke briefly to Allie, then handed the phone to Max. Allie sounded relieved when he told her where Merlin was.

"Well, I'm glad to know he's okay," Allie said to

Max. "I sure wasn't looking forward to telling Jake his best friend was missing."

"Tell Jake we'll take good care of him," Max said. He said goodbye to Allie and hung up the phone.

Max was so anxious to get to the Horse Park, where the equestrian games would take place, that for once he hardly touched his breakfast. He kept trying to rush the other kids and told his father he couldn't have another cup of coffee. But nobody really minded. The other kids were as excited about going to the Olympics as Max was. James Morrison asked for his coffee in a take-out cup, and soon they were on their way.

The Horse Park was on the outskirts of the city, about a half-hour drive from the hotel. When they pulled up to the front entrance, Max's dad had to show a special pass to the security guard.

"Welcome to the Georgia International Horse Park," the guard said, smiling pleasantly. When he had checked out James Morrison's pass and okayed him, he handed them each a plastic card to clip on their clothes. Then he leaned in the window and took a good look at the four kids.

"Y'all have to wear these tags identifying you as visitors at all times while you are in the park. If you're found without your identification tag, you will be escorted from the park. Do you understand?"

"Yessir," Keith said quickly. The others nodded.

"Okay, then." The guard smiled and winked at them. "Enjoy your stay."

"We will!" Max said as they headed up the long driveway toward the group of buildings where the Olympic horses were stabled. As soon as his father parked the Bronco, Max jumped out and hurried toward the largest building, which was a stable. He could see the door to an office inside. It reminded him of the main barn at Thistle Ridge Farm. Beyond the main barn were smaller buildings, which were also stables. They looked new. Max supposed that they must have been built especially for the Olympics.

Keith stood beside Max, looking at the main barn. "Man, this place sure is big," Keith commented.

"It smells just like any barn, though," Max said, catching the scent of a well-kept stable: the sweet-saltiness of horses' bodies and breath mingled with the rich smell of well-oiled leather and clean hay and bedding. Max breathed deeply, beginning to feel at home.

Merlin was sitting at Max's feet, also sniffing the air. All at once, he stood up, intent upon a smell. Before Max could grab his collar, he had run off with his nose in the air, following the scent.

"Merlin!" Max called. "Come back here!" He whistled, but Merlin had vanished behind one of the buildings.

"Shoot!" Max grumbled.

"You'd better go get him, Max," James Morrison said. He had unloaded his equipment and was heading for the office in the main barn. "I'm going to check in and then start taking some photographs."

"We're coming with you, Dad," Megan said. She and Chloe followed him into the main barn.

"Come on, I'll help you find Merlin," Keith said to Max.

The two boys ran after the border collie. Max spotted the white-tipped plume of his tail just as it vanished into one of the smaller barns beyond the main barn.

"There he is," Max said, pointing. "We'd better catch him before somebody complains."

Max and Keith hurried into the barn after Merlin. When Max's eyes adjusted to the light, he saw Merlin standing on his hind legs looking into a stall, his tail wagging happily. The horse inside circled restlessly, snorting nervously at the dog.

"Merlin, come!" Max whistled and patted his thigh. Merlin ran to Max, licked his hand, then ran back to the stall. Max went after him, pulling him down by the collar. "Merlin! Get down!" Max scolded. "You know better than that. You're scaring him!"

As soon as Max had Merlin by the collar, the horse put his head over the stall door. Right away, Max recognized the big chestnut's large, intelligent eyes and the jagged, "broken" blaze on his nose. "Quasar!" Max said fondly. "Keith, look, it's Quasar! Hello, big fella."

Quasar gave Max a friendly shove with his nose, then snorted disdainfully at Merlin. Quasar was a gentle giant, but he didn't like dogs. Max held Merlin by the collar as he and Keith rubbed the big horse's neck. Quasar half closed his eyes and looked as though he would purr if he could.

"Do you think Merlin smelled him from all the way outside?" Max said.

"Dogs have a great sense of smell. And Merlin's one of the smartest dogs I've ever seen," Keith said.

Suddenly, a harsh voice behind Max startled him.

"What are you boys doing in here?" a man said.

Max turned around. A gray-haired man wearing a suit and tie in spite of the heat was peering suspiciously at Keith and Max through wire-rimmed sunglasses. At least, Max assumed he was looking at them; the glasses were the mirror kind that completely hide a person's eyes. Max instantly felt uneasy.

"Well?" the man demanded, stepping forward. "Who let you in here? Let me see your visitors' passes."

Max And Keith showed him the tags clipped to their clothes. He seemed to be reading them very carefully. Then he sniffed loudly. "Visitors are not supposed to have dogs in here."

Max eyed the man. He didn't seem to be a security guard. He wasn't wearing any badge or uniform like the guard at the gate. He had a pass clipped to the lapel of his jacket, but Max couldn't make out the name on it. There was something about the man that made Max suspicious. The man had kept one hand behind his back the whole time they were talking, as if he were hiding something. Max saw him put his closed hand into his jacket pocket. When he took his hand out, it was empty.

"He's not really my dog," Max started to explain. "He's—"

"Then what's he doing here? And what's your business here?"

"I—we—" Max stammered. The man was very unpleasant. Max felt as if he'd been caught doing something forbidden, even though he hadn't.

"Well?"

"They're with me," someone said. "The dog, too."

Another, younger man, wearing riding breeches and broken-in tall boots, was strolling casually toward them. Something about the way he moved seemed catlike to Max, as if springs were coiled under his feet. He looked as if he was ready to leap in any direction. His thick blond hair stuck up in a cowlick over his forehead, then flopped over one eyebrow. He flipped his hair back with a little shake of his head and smiled pleasantly. As he spoke, Max saw the blue of his eyes and the white of his teeth flashing in his handsome face.

"You aren't bothering the man, now, are you, boys?" he asked.

Max wasn't sure if by "the man" he meant Quasar or the man in the suit. But he shook his head anyway.

"I'll keep an eye on 'em, boss," the man in riding clothes said to the man in the suit. "Don't you worry." He winked at the boys and watched the man slyly, chewing slowly on a piece of gum.

"You'd better," the man in the suit said. "And you'll have to leash that dog," he added, shaking his finger at Max.

43

Merlin was looking from one man to the other. He let out a low growl.

"Sorry," Max said, holding Merlin's collar. "I won't let him get loose again," he promised.

The man took out a handkerchief and blew his nose ferociously into it, honking loudly. Max tried not to laugh. He didn't dare look at Keith. The man sniffed several times and put the handkerchief away. He didn't say anything else but went on down the aisle and out the door at the other end of the barn.

The young man rested an elbow on Quasar's stall and lounged against it. He blew a small bubble with his gum, then sucked it in and snapped it loudly in his teeth as Max watched in fascination. The man had deep dimples and a space between his straight, white front teeth that made him look even more handsome. His blue eyes swept over Quasar from his ears to his tail.

"Nice horse," he said appreciatively. Then, without taking his eyes off Quasar, he stuck out a hand for Max and Keith to shake. "Name's Alexander Rance," he said. "Sandy, people call me. Pleased to meet you." He shook the boys' hands. "Care for a stick of gum?" he asked, taking a pack out of his pocket.

Max decided he liked Sandy. "Thanks," he said, taking a stick and handing another to Keith. "I'm Max Morrison, and this is my friend Keith Hill. Do you know Quasar?"

Now Sandy let his eyes slide over to Max. He quit leaning on the stall wall and stood with his hands resting lightly on his hips. "Know him," he said quietly. His eyes moved toward the ceiling. "Know him . . . Hmmm. Now, let me see . . . would a member of the United States Equestrian Team know a horse from the team? Seems to me he would. Yep." He nodded decisively. "I know him. In fact, I'd know Quasar in a herd of a thousand." He reached over and patted Quasar's shoulder vigorously. "You see, ol' Quasar used to belong to me." He grabbed a double handful of Quasar's mane and playfully pushed and pulled the crest of the horse's neck back and forth. "Didn't you, ol' man?" he said to the horse. There was a rough but affectionate manner about the way he touched and spoke to the horse. Then he took his hand off the horse's neck and smiled at Max, his head cocked sideways in a friendly way.

"Then you must know Sharon!" Max exclaimed.

"Sharon!" Sandy exclaimed with delight. Then he frowned. "Sharon who?"

"Sharon *Wyndham*," Max prompted. "She's on the Olympic team? She owns Quasar?" Max said. "*Now*, she owns him," he added, remembering what Sandy had just said.

"Oh, oh, *oh!*" Sandy smacked his forehead with his hand. "You mean *Sharon!* Sharon *Wyndham!* Of *course!*" Sandy nodded soberly. "Yes. I know Sharon. Sharon and I go way back. Now, how do *you* know Sharon?"

"She's our trainer," Max told him. "She owns Thistle Ridge Farm in Hickoryville, Tennessee, where we live."

"She's a great rider," Keith added.

45

"Oh, of course she is," Sandy agreed. "Sharon's one of the best."

"Which team are you on?" Max asked.

"Well, now," Sandy said. "Which do you think?"

Max took another good look at Sandy's clothes and again noticed that he wasn't very tall but that his arms and his thighs were very muscular. He said to Sandy, "Well, you don't look like a jumper rider to me. Those guys are usually more wiry. And you're wearing field boots with laces instead of the dress boots dressage riders wear. I bet you're on the Three-Day team, right?"

"Right you are, junior." Sandy nodded approvingly at Max. "You're a regular brain surgeon, aren't you? Yessirree. A regular little genius."

Max grinned back at him. "I knew it! We have tickets to some of the events. When will you be riding?"

Sandy looked at Quasar again and smiled. "Oh, sooner than you think, boys. Sooner than you think."

Max reached in to stroke Quasar's neck again. "He's beautiful, isn't he, Sandy? Once I got to sit on him."

"No kidding?" Sandy said.

"Yep. Sharon let me get on him and walk him out once. He's so cool."

"He sure is," Sandy agreed.

"Sandy," Keith said, "you said a minute ago that Quasar used to belong to you. How did Sharon end up with him?"

"Yeah," Max said. "Did you sell him? If I had Quasar, I'd never sell him."

Sandy paused before he answered. Then he said,

"No, *I* didn't sell him. I was a victim of circumstance, boys. Do you know what that means?"

"Not exactly," Max admitted.

"Me neither," Keith said.

"It means, boys, that I was *forced* by powers beyond my control to sell Quasar, and three of my other horses. I lost all my money and most of my clients. I almost lost my farm."

"But why?" Max asked.

Sandy searched Max's face as if he were looking for a small spot on a large map. "How old are you?" he asked.

"Eleven," Max answered.

"I'm almost eleven," Keith said.

"Then you might remember the last Olympics. Do you?" Sandy asked them.

"Sure!" Max said. "My sister and I watched the equestrian games at my grandmother's house. We saw Sharon win the silver medal for the United States on Cuckabur."

"*Right!*" Sandy beamed at Max. "You saw Sharon ride. And Greg Miller, and Ian Graham, and Audrey Pendleton. How'm I doing?"

"They were on the jumping team," Max said. "I remember."

"Good, good." Sandy nodded energetically. "You remember them all. But do you remember . . . *me?*" Sandy peered intently at the boys.

Max didn't remember Sandy Rance riding for the United States in those games. Quickly, he looked at Keith, who just shrugged and shook his head. Max

47

tried hard to picture Sandy standing on the platform with the other riders he had named, receiving the silver medal. He didn't want to insult Sandy, but he just couldn't remember him being there.

"Sorry, Sandy, but I can't seem to remember you being there . . . maybe if you remind me what horse you were riding. Was it Quasar?" Max asked hopefully.

Sandy closed his eyes and nodded more slowly. "Yes, yes, Quasar, yes." His eyes snapped open. "Yessirree, bobcat!"

"But I don't remember Quasar being in the Olympics that year," Max said, puzzled.

"That's because he *wasn't!*" Sandy blew a bubble and popped it loudly.

"But I thought you said . . ." Keith trailed off.

"And that's why you don't remember me, either. Because I didn't ride! Your pal Sharon was selected as an alternate that year. She wasn't supposed to be on the team at all. It was supposed to be me and Quasar. But he came up lame the day before we were supposed to compete. He's thrushy, you know?"

Max nodded; he did know what thrush was. He had often seen Sharon treating the bottoms of Quasar's feet with special medication to stop the smelly bacteria from growing and damaging the horse's hooves.

"Quasar was getting over a bad case of it, and he got a big crack in one foot that closed over, and then an abscess developed. That's an infection. It wasn't serious, just bad timing, you understand?" Sandy slung the hair off his forehead again. "Just baaad timing."

"Well, couldn't you ride another horse?" Keith asked.

Sandy gave Keith a sidelong glance. He smiled slightly, but this time no teeth showed. "Now, you're just about as smart as your friend here, you know that?"

Keith couldn't help grinning. Sandy went on. "You should be in charge of the Olympic Committee, instead of those old dudes who are on it. Of *course* I could have ridden another horse," Sandy told them. "I should have been riding Cuckabur. I was older and more experienced than Sharon. I wouldn't have won any old silver medal. It would have been gold all the way for me and any horse I was riding."

"How come you didn't ride, then?" Max asked.

"Because, thanks to the eternal wisdom of the Olympic Committee, no substitutions are permitted. You can only qualify for the team on one horse, and once you make the team, you have to ride the same horse you qualified on. So, if something happens, like it did to Quasar and me, one of the alternate horses and riders goes instead. My horse was lame, so Sharon got to ride Cuckabur in the Olympics, and old Sandy got to soak Quasar's foot in a bucket."

"Wow, that's too bad," Max said. He felt sorry for Sandy. He could just imagine how it would feel to be selected to ride in the Olympics, put in all the training and hard work, and then have to drop out at the last minute.

"I guess it was good for Sharon," Keith pointed out.

"Oh, it was good for Sharon, all right," Sandy agreed. "Yes indeed, it was certainly good for Sharon. But it wasn't too good for Sandy Rance. When I didn't ride, I lost all my endorsements. You know what that means?" With his blue eyes wide open, he watched Max's face.

Max shook his head.

"It means all the corporations who sponsored me to ride in the Olympics withdrew the money they had promised me." Sandy turned around and leaned back against the stall wall again. "Riding is not a cheap sport, boys. Nosirree. I had just spent a big chunk of money on two nice horses—prospects for the next Olympic Games. Then there was a fire in my barn. Not a big one," he assured the boys, "but one of my boarder's horses was hurt badly and had to be put down. This boarder sued me—claimed the fire was my fault. Can you believe that?" Sandy said indignantly. "And, of course, he ended up winning the lawsuit. So I had to come up with a few hundred thousand dollars to pay the damages. To raise the money I had to sell my two best horses. That's how your pal Sharon ended up with Quasar."

"Gosh, it sure sounds like you had a lot of bad things happen all at once," Max said.

"Oh, wait'll you hear the rest. Not long after the lawsuit, one of those nice horses I bought came up from turnout one evening hopping along on three legs. He had smashed one of his front legs somehow, probably from turning too fast or getting kicked by the horse he was turned out with. He had to be put down," Sandy said sadly. "Then, about a month later, the other one had a heart attack! For no good reason at all. They never did find out what caused it." Sandy shook his head sorrowfully. "The vet who did the autopsy said his heart looked perfectly normal."

"Oh, the poor horses," Max said softly. He winced, picturing the animal hobbling around with one leg hanging useless.

"Yes, it was a tragedy," Sandy said. "A terrible tragedy. But fortunately, I had just taken out a large insurance policy on both of the new horses. If it hadn't been for that, I would have been all washed up. Yessir, old Sandy would be mucking out stalls for some two-bit operation if the insurance money hadn't saved me. Insurance is a mighty good thing, boys. When you grow up to be big boys, always carry insurance on your animals," Sandy advised them.

Max had been fascinated with Sandy's tale. Suddenly, Merlin let out a happy whine and lunged away from Max before he could stop him. Max saw the dog running toward a slim woman in riding clothes who had just entered the barn. It was Sharon Wyndham.

5

"HI, SHARON!" MAX CALLED, WAVING.

Sharon approached the boys, trying to calm Merlin at the same time. He was leaping ecstatically around her as she walked, making joyful, throaty little whining noises because he was so happy to see her.

"Sandy, it's Shar—" Max started to say. But Sandy wasn't standing next to Quasar's stall anymore. Max looked around the barn, bewildered.

"That's funny. I wonder why he just disappeared like that," Keith remarked.

"He probably had to groom his horse or something," Max suggested. "You know, he is an Olympic rider. I'm sure he's very busy. It was nice of him to take the time to talk to us."

"Yeah, and he got that grouchy guy to leave us alone," Keith remembered.

"Yeah, I wonder who that guy was," Max said. "He sure was suspicious-looking. He had something behind his back, and he hid it in his pocket. Did you see?"

Keith nodded. Then he made a face as he took the gum out of his mouth. He looked at it and smelled it. "This gum Sandy gave us is weird, isn't it?" He put it back in his mouth.

Max read the gum wrapper. "Teaberry. I never heard of that flavor." He chewed thoughtfully and decided that he liked it. "It's kind of spicy, but it's good."

"Hello, Max and Keith." Sharon Wyndham stood before them, looking every bit the professional rider she was. Her tall black custom-made boots gleamed with polish under a pair of perfectly clean beige breeches. She wore a bright blue polo shirt that exactly matched her eyes, and her golden hair was tucked underneath a very old but very elegant black velvet hunt cap. And, as usual, her lipstick looked as if she had just put it on.

"Hey, Sharon," Keith said.

"Hi, Sharon. How's Quasar been? Does he like it here?" Max asked eagerly.

"Oh, sure. He likes it fine, as long as he's got plenty of hay to snack on. He's been at this barn before, actually. Quasar once belonged to someone from around here." Max saw a peculiar expression flash across Sharon's face for a second, as if she had just tasted something she didn't like at all. But the look vanished as she said, "By the way, I don't suppose either of you could explain to me what Jake's dog is doing here, could you?" Sharon looked at the boys with one eyebrow raised, waiting for them to answer.

When Max told her how they'd discovered the stowaway dog, Sharon's other eyebrow climbed up with the first one. Then she laughed.

"Well, it's a good thing Merlin picked you for his friend, Max," Sharon said, smiling. "For a dog, he's a good judge of character." Then she grew serious as she said, "I heard all about how you and Keith and Megan and Chloe found Jake. You were very brave and very smart. Allie told me you were on Popsicle bareback and that you galloped all the way back to the barn. If you hadn't acted so quickly, Jake might not be alive today. Thank you, Max," Sharon said.

She hugged him very quickly and very hard. When she let him go, Max saw that her eyes were shining brightly. Ordinarily, Max would have felt embarrassed by that kind of attention. But he knew that Sharon didn't give out compliments to people unless she felt they'd really earned it. And he had never seen her hug anybody, except Jake. He felt the same warm feeling that he'd felt when Dr. Pepper had said that Jake would recover from the snakebite.

"It's really Merlin who deserves most of the credit," Max said. "He's the one who led us to Jake."

"He's a good dog," Sharon agreed, scratching Merlin behind the ears. "And he sure loves Jake."

"Will they let you keep him here?" Max asked. "He can't stay in our hotel. My dad's allergic."

"Oh, I guess it'll be all right," Sharon said. "I spotted another dog roaming around here yesterday, and the usual barn cats. Merlin's used to horses, and he's very obedient. I don't think he'll be any trouble. You kids keep an eye on him for me, though, will you? The last thing we need is for Merlin to go trotting through the dressage arena while one of the teams is performing!"

"It's a good thing Earl and Fancy didn't climb into the Bronco, too," Max said. They all laughed at the thought. Earl was Sharon's Jack Russell terrier, and Fancy was the oldest of the barn cats at Thistle Ridge. Fancy and Earl were old enemies; whenever they ran across each other, fur flew!

"Can you imagine if Earl and Fancy got loose in the dressage arena?" Max said.

"I don't even want to think about it," Sharon said.

"Hi, Sharon!" Megan called out, as she and Chloe entered the barn.

"Hello, girls," Sharon said.

"We've been looking all over for you," Megan said to Max and Keith.

"Well, you found us," Keith remarked.

Sharon chuckled. "I was just about to go walk the cross-country course," she said. "Would you four like to come along with me?"

"That'd be great!" Max said.

"Awesome!" Megan said.

"Let's go," Keith said.

They followed Sharon out of the barn, down a hill, and through a clump of trees to the place where the cross-country course began. Other people were also walking the course—the best riders from all nations.

Max spotted a tall, dark-haired man wearing a red shirt with a United States Equestrian Team patch. He tugged on Keith's sleeve. "Keith, isn't that Greg Miller?"

Sharon heard him. "That's him," she said. "Would you like to meet him?"

"Sure!" Max said. Everyone who followed equestrian sports knew and loved Greg Miller and his big white horse, Siberia. Greg and Siberia were always among the top horse-and-rider teams at international competitions.

Sharon went over and spoke to Greg Miller. Seconds later, Max found himself shaking hands with one of the top riders in the world. Greg was very friendly and said that he knew any kid who trained with Sharon Wyndham would end up being a fine rider. He offered to let them meet Siberia later.

"Oh, man, I can't believe we just met *Greg Miller*," Max said in amazement after Greg had excused himself.

"Greg's one of the best," Sharon told the children. "He represents the sport of riding in the best possible way. He's always professional, whether or not he wins. He has deep respect and love for the animal that makes this sport possible, and he always shows it. You never see Greg Miller leave the ring without patting his horse on the neck."

"I always pat my horse," Max said.

"I always pat Bo Peep after we're done working, even if she bucked," Chloe said.

Sharon smiled at her. "I know you do. You're all

great examples for other kids, because you demonstrate good sportsmanship, and you never blame the horse for your mistakes. The very best riders don't ride because they are driven to *win,* they ride because they are driven to excellence."

"Oh!" Max suddenly remembered the discussion they'd had in the car, about the struggle being more important than the triumph. " 'The essential thing is not to have conquered but to have fought well,' " he quoted from the Olympic Creed.

"Exactly," Sharon said.

They went on around the course. As they walked, Sharon explained how the Three-Day team competition was set up. "Each team is tested over three days in three kinds of riding: dressage, speed and endurance, and stadium jumping. On the first day, each team member performs a dressage test. The second day is the hardest. Horses and riders are tested for speed and endurance in a four-part test. The first phase is roads and tracks, where you and your horse are timed over a two- or three-mile course without jumps."

"Like a regular horse race?" Chloe asked.

Sharon nodded. "Then you must ride in a steeplechase. That's a one- to two-mile course around a fenced-in race track with eight or ten brush fences. The third phase is roads and tracks, again, but it's even longer—three to six miles."

"I'm getting tired just listening!" Keith exclaimed.

"But the day still isn't over," Sharon said with a grin. "Finally, you have to ride over the cross-country we're walking right now. This is nearly five miles of up-and-down terrain, with more than twenty jumps."

Sharon paused to check the footing at the base of a huge log jump, while the children exchanged amazed looks.

"You have to do all that in one day?" Max asked. "How do you do it?"

"How do the horses stand it?" Chloe asked.

"Well, obviously you and your horse must be very fit to attempt such a demanding ride," Sharon said, motioning for the children to follow as she headed for the next jump.

"An important part of the test is the veterinary examination," she continued. "The horses are checked carefully before they begin the first day of competition. The roads and tracks and the steeplechase are ridden back to back, with only a one- to two-minute break in between. Then, right before the cross-country phase, there is a mandatory ten-minute halt. Each horse's condition is carefully monitored, and if a horse seems to be in distress, he's not allowed to continue," Sharon explained.

"Oh, that's good," Chloe said, sounding relieved.

"What's on the third day?" Keith wanted to know.

"Stadium jumping," Sharon said. "That's a regular jumper course in an arena, where you're scored on how quickly you can jump the course, and are penalized for knocking down or refusing jumps."

"How do you remember all those courses?" Megan asked in awe. "There are so many fences and this course is so long!"

"Megan, by the time you're skilled enough to make the United States Equestrian Team, memorizing courses isn't usually a problem," Sharon said.

"I never thought of it that way," Megan said.

"A jump course that's well-designed just flows," Sharon said. "Courses are meant to test your ability, but they're also meant to be *rideable*."

"When do you ride, Sharon?" Max asked.

"I'm scheduled to perform my first dressage test for the team score tomorrow," Sharon told him. "The first veterinary inspection is tonight."

"How is the rest of the United States Equestrian team doing so far?" Keith asked.

"The United States team is strong this year in show jumping. We've done well in dressage, but we just never can seem to beat the Europeans. Our Three-Day team is one of the strongest in the world right now, although the English and Canadian teams are excellent. Some of the teams are worried that the high heat and humidity will keep their horses from giving their best performance in the endurance phase. That has been a problem in the past for horses used to cooler climates."

"How do you think Quasar will handle it?" Max asked.

"Oh, Quasar was born and raised in the South. The heat shouldn't bother him. He's used to it," Sharon told him.

They went on around the long course, listening as Sharon explained all the things a rider had to consider when jumping a cross-country course. Max learned that speed was important, but setting a pace that wouldn't tire the horse too soon was the key. The riders really had to know their horses—when to hold back and when to gallop forward. Both horses and riders had to be in excellent physical condition.

Besides the course being long and hilly, the jumps were also challenging. They were mostly natural-looking obstacles, made from wood and brush and stone, but the approaches to the jumps were very tricky. Riders would have to jump uphill or downhill over obstacles on very steep embankments. They would have to jump from high banks down into water, or over jumps positioned in the water, and out again. They would have to jump into a small, fenced-in place and turn very sharply to jump out again. There were penalties for refusals if the horse stopped at a fence or tried to avoid the fence by "running out" around it. If a horse refused three times, the horse and rider were eliminated.

"That's just like in a regular horse show," Chloe pointed out.

"Yes," Sharon said, "except in a regular horse show, a rider who falls off is eliminated. In an endurance test, you can fall off, get back on, and keep riding, as long as you make it over all the obstacles without getting three refusals. But while you're getting back on, the time is still ticking away. And if you fall off a second time, you're eliminated."

"What do you think the hardest part will be?" Max asked. "For Quasar, I mean."

"Quasar's a big marshmallow, as you know," Sharon said. "If he's having a lazy day, I have to really push him to keep the pace. Then I get tired faster. That's the main thing we might have trouble with. I've always been a jumper rider, so I had to work much harder at dressage. But we've put in extra time on it lately, so we ought to make a strong showing."

Max thought Sharon sounded confident, as usual.

By the time they had finished going over the long course with Sharon, the children were tired and hungry. Max was thinking how tired he was from just *walking* the course. How the horses and riders managed to gallop and jump over such a challenging course was amazing to him.

"I've got to be at a team meeting," Sharon said to them. "Can you find your way back to the main barn by yourselves?"

The children said that they could and thanked Sharon for letting them walk the course with her. On the way back, Max spotted Sandy Rance leaving the barn where Quasar was stabled. He waved at Sandy, hoping he would wave back, but Sandy was walking quickly the other way and didn't see him. Then Max saw the older man with the mirrored sunglasses hurrying into the barn. Max wondered again who the man was.

"Who were you waving at, Max?" Megan asked.

"Sandy Rance," Max replied. "Keith and I met him this morning."

Megan frowned. "Who's Sandy Rance?"

"He's on the Olympic team," Max told her. "Don't you know anything?"

"I never heard of him," Megan said.

"Me neither," Chloe said.

"He said he was on the team," Max said.

"He must be an alternate," Chloe suggested.

"Did you know he used to own Quasar?" Max told the girls how Sandy had been cheated out of riding in the last Olympics. They all agreed that it seemed unfair.

In the main barn, they found James Morrison behind a camera set up on a tripod. He was busily snapping pictures of some of the Olympic horses that were stabled there. Later he would use the photographs for reference when he was painting.

Max had seen his dad paint from a photograph. Often, the painting ended up looking more real than the picture. "Why not just be a photographer?" Max had once suggested to his father. "Your paintings look so real, they might as well be photographs. Then you wouldn't have to go to all that trouble."

Max remembered the look his father had given him as he replied, "Max, the challenge for me is to bring out something in the subject I'm painting that looks *more* real than a photograph. The painting is not the trouble. That's the joy. It's the photographs that are work for me."

"Dad," Megan said, "we're *starving*. Can't we go get some lunch now?"

"Soon. I just want to take a few more pictures while

this light is so good. Can you four find something to occupy yourselves with for another half an hour, while I finish up here?" James Morrison asked.

"Okay, Dad," Megan said. "But hurry." She wandered over to a stall at the far end of the barn. A small white head speckled with reddish gray appeared, graced by a pair of dainty, pointed ears and attached to an elegant, arching neck. "Oh!" Megan exclaimed. "Chloe, Max, Keith, look at this little horse!"

The other three kids went to stand by Megan. The horse peered inquisitively at them with large, liquid brown eyes. Its face wasn't flat like most horses but had a little dip in it that made the horse's head seem extra pretty.

"It's an Arabian," Chloe said.

"How can you tell?" Keith asked.

"See its face, how it dips in the middle of its nose? That's called a dish face. It's one of the characteristics of Arabian horses. And look at its tail—see how it's set high and the horse likes to hold it up? That's another Arabian trait," Chloe explained.

"How do you know so much about them?" Keith asked.

Chloe shrugged. "I just finished a book about horse breeds, that's how," she said. "Another interesting thing I learned about Arabians is that they have one fewer vertebra in their spines than other horses. That gives them short, strong backs. Arabians are very versatile, very curious, and very, very smart. In fact, they're one of the most intelligent breeds," Chloe told the others.

"That one looks smart, all right," Megan observed. "I wonder if it's a mare or a gelding." She leaned over and looked. "Mare," she reported, straightening up.

"She's cute," Chloe said.

"What a funny color she is," Max remarked.

The Arabian mare was all white, with tiny, rosy-gray freckles all over her body. The skin around her muzzle and eyes was very dark and felt extra velvety-soft when Max stroked her there.

"She's a flea-bitten gray," Chloe told them.

"How do you know they're flea bites?" Megan asked. "And why would she have so many of them?"

Max, Keith, and Chloe all laughed.

"What's so funny?" Megan asked.

"They're not actual bites from fleas, Megan," Max said.

"They just look all spotty, like little bites," Keith said. "That's where the name comes from."

"Oooh." Megan nodded. "I see."

Max noticed the card on the stall door. Each horse had one, which told its name, a number, and feeding instructions. "It says here her name's Gypsy Rose," Max said. "I wonder what country she belongs to."

"She looks awfully small to be on one of the Olympic teams," Megan said doubtfully. "She might not even be big enough to be a horse. She's not a whole lot bigger than Pixie."

"Yoo-hoo!" a very familiar voice called out. "Ma-ax!"

Max didn't have to look to see who was calling. He would recognize that drawl anywhere. It was Amanda Sloane.

Megan squinted her eyes and made the sort of face she always made when she had to do something she felt squeamish about.

"Oh, no," Max groaned. He wore the exact same expression that was on his sister's face. For once, the two looked very much alike.

"Well, we were bound to run into her sooner or later," Chloe whispered. "We knew she had tickets."

Max remembered the gymkhana show they'd had at Thistle Ridge earlier that summer. He hadn't wanted to be in the gymkhana. But when Megan had been injured and had to drop out, Max replaced her. Max's team—Megan, Amanda, Chloe, and Keith—ended up winning first place. The prize was four tickets to the Olympics. Max had to give his ticket to Megan, since she was really the main team member. He would have been the only one without a ticket if Amanda hadn't offered her ticket to Max in an unusual fit of generosity. She claimed she didn't need it because her father would buy her all the tickets she wanted. Amanda was an only child. Her parents were very wealthy and bought her anything she asked for.

"Hey, Max." Amanda said with a huge smile. Max always noticed the braces on Amanda's perfectly

65

straight teeth. They were the cool, expensive kind that were almost invisible except for the neon-colored bands. Max was going to need braces next year. He hoped his parents would get him the kind Amanda had. He realized Amanda had been saying something to him the whole time he was thinking about the braces. ". . . so glad that I found you here," Amanda finished.

"Uh-huh," Max said. For some reason, Amanda acted bratty and snobbish to all the other kids except Max. He couldn't figure out why. He hardly ever even spoke to Amanda, unless he absolutely had to. Whenever he saw her, he always felt the urge to run away very fast—and sometimes he did. But now he'd have to be nicer to her, because as much as he hated to admit it, he wouldn't be at the Olympics if it hadn't been for Amanda.

"Hello, Amanda," Megan said flatly.

"Hey, Amanda," Chloe said, trying to sound friendly.

"Hey," Amanda said absently. She never paid attention to other people when Max was around. She started talking to Max about how thrilling it was to be at the Olympics and how exciting it was going to be watching Sharon ride, and . . .

Max had quit listening to her. He wished he were somewhere else. Suddenly, he felt Keith elbow him in the ribs. Keith had an amused sparkle in his eyes as he motioned with his head to show Max where to look. What Max saw made him cover his mouth to keep from laughing out loud.

Amanda was standing with her back to Gypsy Rose's stall, going on and on about this and that. Gypsy had her head out over the stall guard, and while Amanda talked, the little horse had been busy. Amanda had two perfect French braids in her blond hair, tied at the ends with yellow satin ribbons that matched her shorts outfit. Max watched as, with her lips, Gypsy deftly untied one of the ribbons and laid it on the floor. Amanda never noticed as Gypsy untied the other ribbon and held it in her teeth, waving it over Amanda's head like a flag.

Finally, Keith and Max couldn't hold back anymore. They began to laugh.

"What's so funny?" Amanda said, smiling.

By then, Megan and Chloe had joined in the laughter. Amanda demanded to know what the joke was. Max was gasping from laughing so hard. He couldn't talk, but he pointed weakly behind Amanda to the little horse, who was still waving the yellow ribbon proudly back and forth.

"Oh!" Amanda squealed when she saw the horse with her hair ribbon. She jumped back as if she'd been bitten, throwing up her hands in alarm. "Oh, my hair bow! Oh, somebody, help! Make it give me back my hair bow—Max! Do something!" Amanda pleaded.

Chloe tried to pull the ribbon from the horse's teeth, but every time she touched it, Gypsy would raise her head, the ribbon dangling just out of reach. Finally, Max stood on tiptoe and managed to get the ribbon. He picked up the other one and handed them over to Amanda.

"I told you Arabian horses were smart," Chloe remarked.

Gypsy seemed to understand her. She nodded her head up and down, as if she were agreeing with Chloe.

"That one isn't," Amanda said huffily. She held out her soggy, dirty hair ribbons in her fingertips. "It's horrible," she said, meaning the horse. Gypsy stretched out her neck toward Amanda and curled her lips in a monkey face, showing her big, blunt yellow teeth. Amanda squealed again and jumped backward. Max and the other kids howled with laughter as Amanda put her hands on her hips and huffed away, pouting.

When they had calmed down, Max wandered outside to wait for his dad. He whistled for Merlin, and in a few moments the dog came running. Max sat down on a patch of grass beside the path and patted the ground next to him. Merlin lay down on his belly, his long pink tongue hanging out. Suddenly, the dog stood up again and barked.

"Shh," Max told the dog. "You'll get yourself in trouble, barking like that." Max decided to walk over and see Quasar. "Come on, Merlin," he called. The dog trotted obediently at his heels as he entered the barn.

Before he'd gotten halfway to Quasar's stall, Max knew something was wrong. There was an uneasiness in the air. One horse whinnied anxiously. Max heard another horse rolling and kicking the walls of its stall. It was Quasar.

Max only had to take one look at the horse's frightened eyes and sweaty, heaving flanks to know that something was terribly wrong with him. He turned around and dashed toward the main barn as fast as he could run.

6

MAX RAN INTO THE BARN. HE TOOK SEVERAL WRONG TURNS before he found his father. "Dad!" he yelled, when he finally spotted him behind the tripod. "Something's happened! We have to call the vet right away!"

"What is it, Max?" his father said.

"It's Quasar! Something's wrong with him! He's down in his stall, and he looks really sick!"

"Now, Max, calm down. It can't be that serious," James Morrison said.

Max ran past his father to the office and yanked open the door without knocking. He ran right into a young woman in a green park ranger's uniform who was on her way out the door. She was tall and sturdy, with dark eyes set in a pleasant face framed by a mass of black hair. Max noticed that the silver name tag pinned under her badge said SALAKS.

"Whoa, slow down there, kid," the ranger said, holding Max by his upper arms. "What's the matter?"

Max was startled. His first instinct was to break away, but when he looked into the woman's face, he saw only kind concern. "I need to call the vet," Max cried. "It's an emergency! One of the horses is sick!"

"Which barn is it?" the ranger said. She unclipped the radio on her utility belt and spoke into it. "Mounted Unit Eighteen to Central Command. Come in, central."

"Proceed, Mounted Eighteen," came the voice over the radio.

"Central, be advised, we have a ninety-three in barn . . ." Ranger Salaks gave Max a questioning look.

Max remembered that the barns were all numbered. For a moment, his mind was a blank, but then he recalled seeing the number two painted over the front door of the building where Quasar was stabled. "Barn two!" Max said. "And tell them to hurry!" he added.

"Two, repeat, barn two," Ranger Salaks said. "Be advised, this is a possible ten-thirteen. Veterinary assistance is requested."

"Ten-four, Mounted Eighteen. Proceed to barn two. Do you require backup?"

"Negative at this time, central. I am proceeding to barn two. Mounted Eighteen out." Ranger Salaks clipped the radio back onto her utility belt. "Show me the horse, kid. Let's go."

Max led Ranger Salaks through the stables as fast as he could. Keith, Megan, and Chloe followed them.

71

When they reached Quasar's stall, the horse wasn't rolling anymore. He lay on his belly, his head up, his nostrils flaring wide with each breath. The veins stood out in his neck and shoulders, and his eyes were wild. He didn't seem to notice when Ranger Salaks opened the door of the stall. She took Quasar's leather halter from its hook on the door and went into his stall.

"Easy, boy," she said in a soothing voice. She approached him cautiously. The big horse seemed to be in a daze. He groaned softly.

"Poor Quasar," Chloe said.

"I wonder what's the matter with him," Megan said.

Max couldn't speak. His stomach was swirling. He realized his fists were clenched so tightly his fingers had gone numb. He uncurled his hands and shook them, opening and closing his fingers until the feeling began to return in hot prickles.

Ranger Salaks almost had the halter over Quasar's head when, without warning, the horse began to thrash around again. The ranger had to jump out of the way of Quasar's flailing hooves as he tried to roll over.

"Ranger Salaks, look!" Max pointed as Quasar squirmed on the floor of the stall, jerking his head angrily. The other side of his neck was bleeding from some kind of wound. "That must be what's upsetting him!"

"I see it," the ranger said tensely. "Holy cow, there's something stuck in there—it looks like a needle! No wonder he's so agitated."

"Can you get it out?" Max asked anxiously.

"I'm going to try, kid," Ranger Salaks reassured him. She stood back until Quasar stopped rolling. The instant he was still, she slipped over to his side and managed to get the halter buckled around his head. Clipping a lead line with a chain shank under his chin, she explained, "We need to get him up, before he gets hurt throwing himself all over the place."

Just then, Quasar squealed angrily and rolled over again. Ranger Salaks stood back but held on to the end of the lead shank. When he was still again, she went to his side. Max thought it was pretty brave of her to go up so close to a horse that was acting so wild. He wasn't sure he could have done the same thing. Quasar looked scary with the whites of his eyes showing and his veins popping out. Max could hardly believe that this was the same gentle horse that he knew and loved.

Ranger Salaks held the lead shank under Quasar's chin and lifted upward. "Come on, boy. Stand up, there," she commanded. He didn't move. She clucked at him and pulled again on the lead shank. "Stand up."

Quasar gave her a look as if he really didn't want to be bothered. He leaned to the side, and for a second Max thought he was going to roll again, but the big horse put his front feet before him, got his hindquarters underneath him, and heaved himself to his feet. He stood still, eyes glazed, neck twitching.

"Good boy," Ranger Salaks said in a kind, calm voice. She stood next to the frightened horse, mur-

muring quietly to him until the vet came. The four kids waited silently.

"What seems to be the problem here?" the vet asked.

Ranger Salaks showed him the wound in Quasar's neck. "Well, I'll be—" The vet looked around at the children and at James Morrison, who stood behind them. "Anybody know how this happened?"

The four kids shook their heads. "My son found him this way, about ten minutes ago," James Morrison explained.

The vet put a hand on Quasar's neck, near the wound. Quasar snorted. He jerked his head up and reared, lifting his front legs off the ground. Ranger Salaks and the vet had to duck out of the way.

"He's pretty upset," Ranger Salaks told the vet. She described how Quasar had been rolling and thrashing around. "You may need to twitch him."

"Well, we'd better get him out of this stall, before one of us gets stepped on," the vet said.

Ranger Salaks led Quasar out of the stall. The vet took out a "twitch," a wooden-handled tool with a short chain loop at the end. Max knew a twitch was used for getting feisty horses to stand still for a few minutes. He watched as the vet pulled Quasar's upper lip out, slipped the chain around it, and twisted the handle until the chain held the horse's lip firmly. Most horses wouldn't fight with their lip held like that, Max knew. When used properly, a twitch wouldn't injure the horse's lip. It was a good way to keep an excited horse standing still.

The ranger held the lead shank and the handle of the twitch, while the vet took a pair of forceps from his bag and closed them on the end of the needle sticking out of Quasar's neck. Quasar snorted when he felt the vet touch the sore place. He started to jerk his head up but felt the twitch and was still again, except for his eyes, as he looked around fearfully. When the vet saw that Quasar would stand quietly, he deftly pulled out the needle.

The horse grunted but then relaxed immediately when the needle came out of his neck. Blood spurted, then trickled from the wound. Max sighed with relief.

The vet examined the puncture and then cleaned it. He was just bandaging it when Sharon hurried in.

"What happened?" Sharon said. "A groom told me Quasar was hurt. What's the matter with him?"

Ranger Salaks and the vet told her how they'd found Quasar. While they were explaining, Max wandered into Quasar's stall. The fluffy wood shavings used for bedding were churned up and mixed with Quasar's hay. The horse had kicked his water bucket and overturned it, wetting one side of the stall. Max walked slowly around the area, his eyes glued to the floor, looking for some kind of clue that might explain what had happened to Quasar.

He stirred the bedding with the toe of one sneaker. Something pink caught his eye. Max picked it up, hoping it was a clue, but it was only a piece of gum. He tossed it aside, wiping his hand on his shorts as he continued to search the floor. Suddenly, he spotted something. He bent down and gingerly picked it up. It was a plastic syringe, three-quarters filled with a clear fluid.

"But how could he have gotten a needle stuck in his neck?" Sharon was saying. "Unless—"

"Look, you guys!" Max said excitedly as he came out of Quasar's stall. He held out the syringe.

"What have you got there, Max?" James Morrison said curiously.

"Let me see that," the vet said, taking the syringe from Max. He examined it carefully. Then he compared it with the needle he had found in the horse's neck. The tiny stub of needle left in the syringe fit exactly with the broken end of the bent needle he'd pulled from Quasar's neck. The vet held the two ends together and showed Sharon. The adults looked at each other. Sharon's expression was alarmed.

"It looks like somebody was trying to hurt your horse," the vet said grimly.

There was a shocked silence. Then Sharon said, "What's in the syringe?"

The vet said, "I can't be positive until I take this back to my lab and run an analysis on it, but it seems to be . . ." He paused when he realized all the kids were looking at him. Then he pulled Sharon aside and went on speaking quietly to her.

Max couldn't hear what the vet was saying, but he heard Sharon draw in her breath sharply, exclaiming, "But that's ridiculous! Of course I didn't do it! And why would someone else try to drug my horse, unless . . ." Sharon broke off, and both her eyebrows shot upward as she looked at the vet, speechless.

"Unless they wanted you to fail the veterinary inspection," the vet finished for her. "It looks like someone was trying to make it look like you gave your horse a little something to perk him up."

"But the committee is going to test the horses tonight!" Sharon said. "What if Quasar doesn't pass? They'll think I drugged him, to boost his energy level and make him run faster in the cross-country event. Drugging the horses is illegal—I could be disqualified from the team!"

The vet nodded soberly. "Yes, you certainly could. And it seems that that's exactly what someone was trying to do."

"But who would want to do that to Quasar and Sharon?" Max protested. "And why?"

"That's the mystery," the vet said, shaking his head. Max watched as he put the needle and the syringe into a plastic bag and sealed it carefully. "Obviously whoever tried to do this almost got caught in the act and had to run away quickly. Maybe your horse didn't get enough of the drug in his bloodstream to register on the test. Good luck," the vet said sympathetically.

"Please let me know as soon as you find out exactly what was in the syringe," Sharon said. She stroked her horse's neck. Quasar was standing quietly, now that there was no needle in his neck to aggravate him. Max was relieved to see the horse acting like his old self again.

Sharon led Quasar back into his stall and closed

the door. A groom had already replaced the hay, put down fresh bedding over the wet place, and refilled the water bucket. Sharon smiled as she observed, "These grooms are almost as good as Allie."

"I'll have to report this to the Parks Department," Ranger Salaks informed them. "And to Olympic Security." She began questioning Sharon, writing down the answers in a notebook. Then the ranger turned to Max and asked, "What's your name, kid?"

"Max Morrison." He answered a few more questions, then Ranger Salaks closed her notebook. She took out her radio again and called headquarters.

"Max," Sharon said, "are you sure you didn't see *anyone* around when you found Quasar? It's hard to believe there wasn't even a groom in here."

Max thought hard. "Nooo . . . I don't remember seeing anyone. I just remember hearing a lot of commotion coming from the stall, and then I found Quasar acting all crazy. After that I ran back to the main barn and told Ranger Salaks." Max looked up at the ranger.

"You did the right thing, kid." She smiled at him.

"You certainly did," Sharon agreed. "I've got to go and talk to the team captain. If you kids see *anything* suspicious while you're around the barn, be sure to tell me or a park ranger, okay?"

Max, Keith, Megan, and Chloe all promised that they would be on the lookout for anything out of the ordinary. James Morrison went to finish loading up his camera and equipment. The children promised to meet him at the Bronco in fifteen minutes.

"Did you call yourself 'Mounted Eighteen' on your radio?" Max asked the ranger.

"Yep. Mounted Eighteen—that's me," the ranger said.

"But you're not mounted," Keith pointed out.

"Not right now, I'm not. But I am usually on mounted patrol. This is a huge park; it's more than a thousand acres. We have some officers on foot patrol, but most of the rangers are on horseback. That way, we can cover more territory faster. I'm Mounted Eighteen whether I'm actually on my horse or just at lunch," she explained.

"Ranger Salaks, where's your horse?" Megan asked.

"Why don't you all call me Tina?" the ranger said. "And what are your names?"

Megan, Chloe, and Keith introduced themselves. They all wanted to see Tina's horse, so she led them up to the main barn. In the stall next to Gypsy Rose was a big reddish-brown horse. Tina pointed to him, saying, "This is Mounty."

Mounty was very tall, with a broad back and a wide, round rump. His mane was a few shades lighter than his coat and stood straight up on the crest of his arched neck. He had huge feet with long tufts of fur at the backs of his ankles. Max thought he and his sister and their friends could have easily fit on his back all at once, with room for more!

Mounty stuck his head out over the stall guard, and Tina patted him. She unwrapped a piece of red and white striped hard candy and fed it to him.

"My pony loves breath mints," Megan told Tina.

"Mounty loves peppermints," Tina said. The big horse crunched on the candy and then nosed around, looking for more. "That's all you get, Mou," Tina said.

Gypsy Rose stuck her little head over the stall guard and reached around toward Mounty. The bigger horse responded by touching noses gently with the little mare.

"Aw, they look like they're kissing," Megan said.

Tina smiled. "Gypsy and Mounty are best friends. Gypsy belongs to one of the caretakers here at the park. Her owner tried to move her out to one of the new barns while the Olympic horses were here, but she pitched such a fit he had to bring her back. She's old and has been in this stall for a very long time. Mounty was glad when she came back. Gypsy's your girlfriend, isn't she, Mou?" Tina rubbed her horse's neck.

"He's really pretty," Chloe said. "Is he a draft horse?"

"Yes."

"I thought so." Chloe nodded. "He's so big, and he has those tufts of long hair at his ankles."

"How tall is he?" Max asked.

"He's seventeen hands, two inches," Tina said.

"Wow, almost as tall as Quasar," Max said. "How many hours a day do you ride him?"

Tina explained, "We go out on a morning shift for about four or five hours. Then we come in for a couple of hours so we can both have lunch. Then, about two o'clock, we head out again. The park closes at dusk, so we're usually back in the late evening."

"Boy, you really ride a lot," Keith said. "Doesn't your seat get tired?"

Tina gave him an amused look. "Not really. The saddle is big and comfortable for both of us."

Mounty wore his saddle in his stall. It was a very large black leather saddle. Max noticed it was shaped more square than an English saddle and even larger than a western saddle. And the stirrups were English stirrups. There was a large, fluffy square pad under the saddle, with the park ranger's logo embroidered near the back corners.

"What kind of saddle is that?" Max asked. "I never saw one like it."

"It's a cavalry saddle," Tina said. "Mounted officers are trained to ride cavalry style when they are at the academy. That's how the military used to train its mounted soldiers."

"Oh, I've seen old movies where they ride like that," Keith said.

"Is it more like English or western?" Megan asked. "The saddle looks like a mixture of both."

"That's a good observation," Tina said. "Cavalry-style riding does combine elements of both English and western riding."

"Do you post when you trot?" Chloe wanted to know.

"Yes. And we use English bridles and bits, but we steer with both neck rein and direct rein. Our horses have to be trained to respond to both, because sometimes we have to use the radio or write up a summons with one hand and still be able to guide the

81

horse with the other." As she spoke, Tina took down Mounty's bridle from the hook on the door and began to put it on him. The leather straps were thick and heavy. There were big shiny brass fittings where the brow band joined the cavesson on either side of Mounty's head, and shiny brass buckles on the cheek pieces and the throat latch.

"He looks so handsome in it," Megan said.

"Don't the horses get tired from carrying around those big, heavy saddles all day?" Chloe asked. "It seems like they would let you use a smaller, lighter saddle for riding so many hours."

"That's a good point, Chloe. But the fact is, your little English saddles put most of the rider's weight over a very small part of the horse's back. Our saddles are large, but they're pretty light for their size. They're meant to spread out the weight of the rider over a larger area of the horse's back, which is better for horses who spend long hours under saddle," Tina explained.

"Oh, that makes sense," Chloe said.

"A saddle like that would cover up Pixie's whole back!" Megan said, giggling at the thought.

"Pixie would never let a saddle like that anywhere near her!" Max said. "She'd spook and run away."

"True," Megan admitted.

Tina had finished tacking Mounty. She led him out of his stall and down the aisle. The kids followed, watching as she put on her helmet and mounted up. "Well, we're off," she said. "See you soon."

" 'Bye, Tina!" they called. She waved at them, then trotted off, following a path through the park.

"I bet that's a fun job," Keith said. "Maybe I'll be a park ranger when I grow up."

"Max! Megan!" James Morrison called to them from the parking lot near the barn. "Come on!"

"Let's go," Megan said. "I'm starving!"

At lunch the children talked and talked about the strange incident involving Quasar. "But why would anybody want Sharon to be disqualified?" Max kept saying. "I just don't understand it."

"There are some people in the world who are only interested in helping themselves," James Morrison explained. "Those people usually feel unhappy with their own lives, so they never want anybody else to succeed, either. That's the sort of person who would try to hurt Quasar or keep Sharon from riding. Maybe it's someone from another team, who thinks Sharon could beat them. Maybe it's a groom who doesn't like Sharon for some reason. We may never know. It's just a good thing whoever tried to hurt Quasar didn't succeed."

"Well, I'm going to watch him like a hawk," Max said determinedly. "Nobody's going to hurt Quasar while I'm around."

"I'm with you, Max," Keith said.

"We'll help, too," Megan said.

Chloe added, "We'll be the Short Stirrup Rangers!"

"Yeah!" Max said. "We can take turns guarding Quasar and searching for clues. I found the syringe in his stall. Maybe there are more clues. Maybe we can discover who tried to hurt him."

"Short Stirrup Rangers, to the rescue!" Keith said. He put out a hand, and Megan, Chloe, and Max piled their own hands on top.

"Do any of you Rangers have time for dessert?" James Morrison wanted to know.

"Strawberry pie!" the girls said. At the same time, the boys yelled, "Hot fudge brownies!"

"Two strawberry pies, two hot fudge brownies, and a coffee," James Morrison told the waitperson.

"And the check, please," Max added. "As soon as we finish dessert, we have to get to work!"

7

WHILE JAMES MORRISON SPENT THE REST OF THE DAY taking pictures in the afternoon light, the Short Stirrup Rangers took turns keeping watch by Quasar's stall. Whoever wasn't on watch went searching for clues. Max was sure that if they kept on looking, eventually something would turn up.

After a few hours, though, everyone was getting tired. It was boring just sitting by Quasar's stall. And even after each of them had been all over the barns and the grounds nearby, nothing suspicious had turned up—not even a footprint.

"Hey, Max," someone said.

Max looked up and saw Amanda Sloane mincing toward him. He groaned inwardly but managed a polite smile. "Hello, Amanda," he said. Then he continued to walk with his head down, searching the ground, hoping she would leave him alone.

"I've been watching the dressage finals," Amanda said. She yawned daintily. "But it's sooo boring. So I told Mama and Daddy I was going to wait for them over here. What are you doing?"

"I'm looking for clues," Max said.

"Clues?" Amanda said curiously, lowering her gaze as she began to walk beside him.

"Yes. Didn't you hear about what happened to Quasar this morning?" Max said.

"No. What happened?" Amanda asked.

"Somebody tried to inject something into him. He had a needle broken off in his neck, and I found a syringe on the floor of his stall," Max told her.

"Well, maybe the vet did it," Amanda said.

"Nope." Max shook his head firmly. "It was definitely *foul play*," he said, lowering his voice dramatically.

"What was in the syringe?" Amanda asked.

"I don't know," Max admitted. "The vet said he had to test it in the lab. But the Olympic Committee examines the horses to be sure nobody is giving them drugs to make them go faster or calm them down. If they find anything in Quasar's blood, he and Sharon could be banned from competing in the Olympics."

"Well, if anything happens to one of the main team members, they let one of the alternates ride instead," Amanda said.

"I know that," Max said.

"My daddy sponsors one of the alternate riders. His name is Sandy Rance," Amanda said smugly. "My daddy says Sandy is by far the most talented rider on the Three-Day team."

"I know Sandy," Max said. "He's cool. Have you met him?"

"Well, of course I have," Amanda said airily. "He's been over to our house for dinner many times. Perhaps you would like to join us one night."

"Is that really true?" Max asked skeptically. Amanda was always inviting him over for dinner, and he was always making excuses for why he couldn't go. She might just be making up the story about Sandy having dinner at her house so that Max would finally agree to come over.

Amanda put her hands on her hips. "Of course it's true," she insisted. "He's a very good friend of my father's. I've seen him plenty of times."

Max thought about it. He knew Amanda's father had a lot of money. Maybe it was true. It would be cool to have dinner with Sandy Rance. "Well . . . maybe," Max said. He decided the next time he spoke to Sandy, he would ask him if he knew the Sloanes.

Just then, they saw Sandy come out of the main barn leading a pretty black mare. "Well, if it isn't Max-a-million. And Amanda-panda! Hey there, kiddies," Sandy said.

"Hey, Sandy," Amanda said, in the simpering way she always spoke to grown-ups or people she might get something out of. To Max, she said smugly, "I *told* you I knew him."

"Hi, Sandy," Max said, doing his best to ignore Amanda. He hoped Sandy wouldn't get the idea that he and Amanda hung out together or something. "Is this your horse?" he asked, stepping toward them and away from Amanda.

"Yep," Sandy said. "This is Marauder. But I call her Maude, don't I, Miss Maude?" Sandy slapped the mare's neck affectionately.

"She sure is big for a mare," Max said, admiring the beautiful horse. She had a perfect white diamond on her forehead and one white sock on her right hind foot.

"She sure is. You sure have got an eye for horses," Sandy exclaimed. "Well, I'm off. Ol' Maude and I have a little schooling to take care of, don't we, Maude?" He looked the horse in the eye. "See you later, kiddies." He winked at Max and headed for the schooling ring, leading the horse.

" 'Bye, Sandy," Max said, waving.

"My father bought Sandy's horse for him," Amanda bragged. "She's a Dutch Oldenberg mare, and she cost six hundred thousand dollars. He thinks that Sandy can make him a whole bunch of money riding her in the big shows. But, of course, he's really thrilled that Sandy and Marauder made it to the Olympics this year. Daddy's hoping Sandy will end up getting to ride," Amanda said.

"But, Amanda, for Sandy to get to ride, one of the team members would have to be disqualified," Max protested.

Amanda shrugged. "So?"

Max frowned at her. "Amanda, what if you were on the Olympic team? Wouldn't you feel bad if you had put in all that training, and someone else ended up getting to ride instead of you?"

Amanda flipped her yellow braids behind her shoulders with a toss of her head. "Well, what if you were the alternate rider, and you ended up getting to ride? Wouldn't you be glad?" she asked.

Max made a face. Amanda had a point. And Max remembered that in the last Olympics, Sharon had been an alternate but then had gotten to ride. "Well, if one of the alternates does get to ride, it's not going to be because Sharon and Quasar *don't* get to ride," Max vowed. "Not if I can help it."

"Can I help y'all search for clues?" Amanda begged.

Max thought about it. He knew the other kids wouldn't want Amanda hanging around. He didn't, either. But one more person would help keep Quasar safe, even if it was Amanda.

"I guess so," Max said. "Start looking, then. And let me know if you find *anything*. Even a small clue could be important."

A moment later, Max saw Tina, the park ranger, coming down a path that led out of a wooded section of the park. He waved at her, and she waved back. She was with another officer riding a big black-and-white spotted leopard Appaloosa.

"Hey, Max," Tina said, jumping off Mounty. "Who's your friend?"

"I am Amanda Susannah Sloane," Amanda said primly.

Amanda always introduced herself by her whole name. Max thought that was so weird. His whole name was Maxwell James Morrison, but he didn't want anyone to know that "Max" really stood for "Maxwell." But he hadn't minded when Sandy called him "Max-a-million." He kind of liked that.

"What a cool horse," Max said to the ranger on the Appaloosa. The blue-eyed horse was looking grandly at Max. He thought that if the horse could talk, he would be saying, "Well? Am I not the most beautiful Appaloosa horse you have ever seen on this whole entire planet?"

"This is Fritz," the other ranger said. "And I'm Lori. Tina and I are partners."

"My horse has blue eyes, too," Max said. He patted Fritz, who snorted proudly.

"What are you kids doing?" Tina asked.

"We're being detectives," Max explained. "We're going to keep searching this place until we discover who tried to hurt Quasar."

"Good," Tina said, smiling. "Let us know if you find anything."

"Yeah," Lori said, jumping off Fritz. "We'll be on the case in a second."

"Don't worry," Max said. "The Short Stirrup Rangers are on the trail of the criminal. We'll catch him, whoever he is."

The park rangers said goodbye and led their horses into the stables. Max started to show Amanda how to search the ground. "We're looking for evidence," he told her. "Especially footprints and stuff like that. We could find out who the criminal is if we found his actual footprints."

"But there are so many footprints," Amanda complained. "How would you know which footprints belonged to a criminal?"

"You just know." Max sighed. He didn't think Amanda was going to make a very good detective. She didn't listen to his instructions, and kept jabbering about this and that and looking everywhere but at the ground.

"Max, look over there at that man," Amanda said, pointing.

Max was busy examining the ground under the window behind Quasar's stall. "Amanda, I told you, if you want to be a Short Stirrup Ranger, you have to be quiet and search for clues. What if we miss something because you were talking?" he said impatiently.

"Well, what if you're so busy looking at the ground you miss an important clue that's walking right by you?" Amanda said.

Max looked up. At the far end of the barn, he saw the man with the mirrored sunglasses walking quickly toward a silver car. He was carrying a handful of syringes!

"Amanda, is that the man you were talking about?" Max asked, lowering his voice.

"Yes," Amanda said. She put her hands on her hips and tossed her braids back again. "I tried to tell you about him a while ago. I saw him go into the barn, then he came out with all those syringes. Next time, maybe you'll listen to me when I tell you something," Amanda said prissily.

"Well, why didn't you say so in the first place?" Max said. "I bet that's the bad guy!" The man opened his car door and got in. Max knew he'd have to act fast. He told Amanda. "Stay here and watch him. I'm going to get Tina."

Max tore up the path to the barn as fast as he could. He found Tina outside Mounty's stall. She had taken off his bridle and was about to unsaddle him. "Tina!" Max said. "Listen—!" He told her about the suspicious man he and Amanda had seen leaving the barn.

"Where is he now?" Tina demanded, pulling out her radio. Max described the man's car as Tina called in the description to the ranger's headquarters. Then she quickly put Mounty's bridle back on, led him outside, and swung up into the saddle.

"This way," Max said. He led Tina to the side of the barn where Amanda was waiting. "Amanda, where is he?" Max said, panting.

Amanda pointed down the long driveway. "He got in the car and drove away, that way. He turned off the driveway to the right, but I didn't see which way he went after that."

"Come on, then," she said to Max, putting out a hand. "You'll have to show me the guy." She pulled Max up behind her on Mounty's broad back. Then she took off her helmet and gave it to him. As soon as he had buckled it securely, they were off.

Max held on to the back of Tina's belt with both hands as they cantered up the driveway in the direction Amanda had pointed. Mounty didn't seem to mind carrying an extra person. At first, Max was anxious that he might slip sideways, but soon he was used to Mounty's canter. It was smooth and easy to sit to. And it was really thrilling to be chasing after a real live bad guy on horseback, just like a sheriff in a cowboy movie! Max even took one hand off Tina's belt and put it on his thigh, ready to draw his six-shooter when they caught the outlaw, the way he had seen them ride in the movies.

At the end of the driveway, Tina turned Mounty and followed a narrow paved road. Soon they spotted the silver car, which was moving slowly.

"There he is!" Max pointed.

Tina grabbed her radio again as they came closer to the car. "Mounted Eighteen to Central, be advised, we have the perpetrator in sight."

"Do you need backup?" said the voice on the radio.

"Negative. Be advised, I am ten-ten at this time, Central. Stand by."

"Ten-four."

"What's ten-ten?" Max asked her as they caught up with the car.

"That means I'm investigating a situation," Tina explained to Max. As they drew up behind the vehicle, she brought Mounty down to a trot. To the driver, she called out in a loud, authoritative voice, "Stop the car!" The car stopped, its engine running. The driver did not get out.

"Can you hold Mounty?" Tina asked Max, pulling Mounty to a halt behind the car.

"Sure I can," Max replied. He and Tina dismounted.

Max held Mounty by the reins while Tina went to the car. *We've got him now,* Max was thinking. He felt very important and proud to have led Tina right to the bad guy. *Wait till I tell Keith about this!* he thought.

The driver rolled down his window. Max caught a glimpse of the side of the man's face. He still wore his mirrored sunglasses, even though it was late in the evening.

Max saw the man hand Tina a small business card. She read it and after speaking a few words to the driver, handed it back. The man rolled up the window and drove away. Tina walked back to Max and Mounty.

"You let him go?" Max said in amazement. "But, Tina, that's the guy! He's the one Amanda and I saw leaving the barn with all those syringes. And I saw him before, too," Max remembered. "Keith and I caught him at Quasar's stall this morning, and he tried to act like *we* were doing something wrong. I saw him hide something in his pocket—I'll bet it was the syringe! I'll bet you anything he was going to do something to Quasar then, and we just happened to catch . . . him . . ."

Max realized that Tina was glaring at him. "What's the matter?" Max asked nervously. "Why are you looking at me like that?"

Tina put her fists on her hips and said, "Do you know who that guy is? He's no criminal. He's one of the officials on the Inspection Panel for the equestrian games! Do you know how much trouble I'm going to be in when my supervisor finds out I was in hot pursuit of an Olympic official?" she demanded. "You don't make up stories about people unless you're positive you saw them doing something wrong!"

"But why was he carrying all those syringes from the barn to his car, then?" Max protested. "Did you ask him that?"

"Because he's in charge of the routine drug testing the Inspection Panel performs on all the Olympic horses. They're testing tonight. He was carrying the samples to the lab for analysis!" Tina said.

"Oh," was all Max could say.

Tina took Mounty's reins from Max and mounted up. "Come on," she said, offering Max a hand.

He scrambled up behind her and sat quietly while they walked back to the Olympic stables, feeling embarrassed. Detective work was harder than he had thought.

When they were nearly to the stables, Max said, "I'm really sorry for making you chase after that man, Tina. We were just so sure he was the bad guy."

"Oh, I know you are," Tina said. "Just do me a favor. The next time you think you're on the trail of a criminal, be sure you actually saw him commit a crime first, okay?"

"Okay," Max said sheepishly.

After dinner, Max, Megan, Keith, and Chloe sat on the girls' bed talking about the day. Max was disappointed that they hadn't been able to catch the person who had tried to drug Quasar. "At least Quasar wasn't disqualified, though," Max said. Earlier Sharon had told them that nothing questionable had turned up in Quasar's blood. Everyone was relieved, especially Sharon.

"The Three-Day event begins tomorrow," Megan said. "I can't wait to watch Sharon ride. It's going to be so exciting."

"I wonder what Sharon does the night before a big show like this," Chloe mused. "Do you think she's nervous?"

"I doubt it," Megan said. "Sharon never gets upset about anything."

"Besides," Keith added, "she's been in the Olympics twice before. She's probably used to it by now."

"I wish I could be like that," Chloe said. "I can't even eat dinner the night before a horse show."

"I can," Keith said. "I eat even more dinner than usual the night before a horse show. Even thinking about horse shows makes me hungry!"

"You guys," Max said. "I just thought of something. Somebody really wanted to stop Sharon and Quasar from competing tomorrow."

"Yeah, but they didn't," Megan said.

"They didn't today. But whoever it was might try again," Max said.

"But the event starts tomorrow. It's too late to do anything about it," Keith said.

Max shook his head and said worriedly, "Somebody wanted Sharon disqualified, enough to risk getting caught messing with Quasar in broad daylight. They didn't succeed today, but what if they decide to try again—*tonight?*"

Everyone thought about that. "Max could be right," Chloe finally said.

"Tina told me guards patrol the stables at night," Keith said. "Don't you think they would catch anybody who tried to sneak in?"

"Someone got into Quasar's stall in the middle of the day without getting caught. Don't you think it would be even easier at night?" Max asked.

"Well, what can we do about it?" Megan asked.

Max glanced toward the adjoining room, to be sure his father wasn't paying attention to them. James Morrison had dozed off in front of the television. "We can guard Quasar ourselves," Max said in a loud whisper.

"How?" Keith asked.

"We'll go back to the barn and keep watch over him all night," Max said. "That way, if anyone tries to bother him, we can sound the alarm."

"Dad will never let us go out this late at night," Megan said.

"Dad's asleep already," Max said, pointing at the bed in the other room. The four kids peered through the door at James Morrison, who was snoring softly. "We can slip out, stay until early morning, then be back before he wakes up. You know what a sound sleeper he is," Max said.

Megan giggled. "You're right," she whispered. "We could probably drive a truck through the room without waking him up."

Max looked earnestly at his sister and his friends. "Are you with me, then?" he asked them.

They all nodded. Max put out a hand. The other kids piled their hands on top. "Short Stirrup Club!" they chanted in a whisper.

Megan went to the bed she shared with Chloe and began stuffing the pillows under the covers.

"Megan, what are you doing?" Max asked her. "We have to get going."

"I'm making it look like we're in bed asleep," she explained, arranging the pillows. "That way, if Dad does decide to check on us, he won't notice we're gone."

"Good thinking, Bucket Head," Max said admiringly.

"Thanks, Manure Brain," Megan replied.

The boys quietly arranged their own bed the same way. Then they turned off the lights and started out. The door squeaked when Megan opened it. They all stopped and held their breath as James Morrison stirred, then muttered something. When he seemed to be sleeping soundly, Max motioned for the other kids to go on out of the room. He had spotted his father's Polaroid camera on the dresser next to the door. His dad used it to take test shots before he photographed his subjects with the 35-millimeter camera. Max had a hand on the camera when his father spoke.

"What's the matter, Max?" he said.

Max was so startled he nearly dropped the camera,

but he managed to answer calmly. "Nothing, Dad," he said. "I was just locking the door."

"Are the other kids asleep?"

Max hesitated, trying to think how to answer without actually telling a lie. "They're ... out for the night," he told his dad.

"Good," James Morrison said. "Max, can you turn off the television? Thanks."

"You're welcome. Good night, Dad," Max said. He stood absolutely still in the dark room and waited, holding his breath. In a few moments, he heard his father snoring again. He picked up the camera, tiptoed to the door, and squeezed through the smallest opening he could, so it wouldn't squeak again. Then he closed it very slowly behind him. There was a soft *click* as the latch caught, and Max sighed with relief.

Megan, Chloe, and Keith were waiting by the elevator. "Boy, was that a close call!" Max exclaimed.

"Is he asleep?" Megan asked.

"Yes," Max said.

"What's the camera for?" Keith said, pointing to the Polaroid Max wore over his shoulder.

"For photo evidence." Max grinned. "In case we spot the bad guy. This time, we can take pictures to back up our story."

"Good idea!" Keith said approvingly.

Max nodded. "Let's go," he said.

When they were outside the hotel, Keith said, "By the way—how are we going to get to the Horse Park?"

Max frowned. He hadn't thought of that. They could call a cab, but it would cost a lot of money to go that far. "I guess we have to walk," he said doubtfully.

"No way," Keith said, shaking his head. "I'm not walking all the way to the stables. Not through a strange city at night."

"I know how we can get there," Chloe said. "Atlanta has a very good public transportation system. There's a bus that goes right to the Horse Park. I read about it in the Olympic guide book I picked up at the front desk."

"Chloe, you're awesome!" Max said with admiration.

"Where can we catch the bus?" Megan asked.

Chloe pointed to a lighted bus stop just down the street. "I think it stops right there," she said.

A bus was coming down the street as she spoke. "Come on!" Max said, and they ran to the end of the block. They made it to the stop just as the bus was leaving. The driver braked and opened the doors again, and the four children climbed on. They sat down, and the doors closed with a hiss as the bus pulled away. Max relaxed in his seat. So far the plan was working. No one would keep Sharon from riding the next day, as long as the Short Stirrup Club was there to protect Quasar!

8

THE BUS LET THE CHILDREN OFF NEAR THE ENTRANCE TO the Horse Park after a twenty-minute ride, just as Chloe had said it would. The entrance and the driveway were well lit. A sign on the front gate said that no visitors were permitted in the park after dark. But the gate was really meant to keep cars out, so there was room to crawl under it easily. They all scrambled under it and made their way up the drive.

There was a light in the guardhouse, about twenty yards from the gate. They bent low and scurried past it, keeping to the shadows by the edge of the road. Max caught a glimpse of the security guard inside reading a novel and drinking a soda. He turned a page as they sneaked by but did not look up.

Soon they had made their way to the stables. The grounds were dark, except for the outside lights over the door of each barn. Max also saw a light in the park rangers' office in the main barn. He wondered if Tina was inside.

They were just about to enter barn two when they heard footsteps coming down the aisle toward them. They froze, flattening themselves against the wall of the building. Someone came out of the barn, and Max breathed a sigh of relief. It was only a security guard, patrolling the area. He headed toward one of the other barns.

"Now," Max whispered. They tiptoed inside and stood for a minute, trying to get their bearings in the dim light. There was a sort of alcove across from Quasar's stall that had once been another stall. The front wall had been removed, and bales of cedar shavings, used for bedding in the stalls, were stacked there. It would be a perfect place to keep watch, Max decided. They could easily hide among the bales, which were deep in the shadows, but they had a good view of the front entrance and of Quasar's stall. After checking on the horse, they climbed among the bales and settled down to watch.

For a while, they whispered together. When a guard walked through the barn, they kept absolutely still and silent. The guard never saw them. Max tried to read his watch and made out that it was two-thirty. He yawned for the third time in the last minute. He could see Keith nearby, blinking his eyes like an owl in the darkness, trying to stay awake. Chloe and Megan had fallen asleep on the bales of shavings. The next time he looked at Keith, his eyes were closed, too, and his head drooped on his chest. Max rubbed his eyes hard and sat up straighter. He was getting sleepy, but he was determined to stay awake.

All was quiet except for the normal sounds of horses moving in their stalls at night. But with everyone else asleep, Max felt a little lonely. Once he heard an ominous flutter overhead that sounded like a bat. He shuddered, wondering at how the most friendly and familiar places could seem so strange and scary in the darkness.

Suddenly, Max heard a clicking sound, followed by soft panting. He listened hard. The sound came closer until it seemed to stop right in front of him. Max was getting scared. Should he wake Keith? But something was there—some *thing*, he realized. Maybe if he didn't move, it wouldn't notice him. Max strained his eyes, trying to see through the shadows, and felt something wet and warm on his hand. He jerked it back and gasped. Then a familiar, furry body was rubbing against him. "Merlin!" he whispered. "Am I glad to see you!"

The friendly dog licked Max's chin in greeting, then settled down on a bale at Max's side. Max laid a hand on the dog's head and stroked him reassuringly. But it was really himself he was reassuring, he knew. He tried hard to stay awake but his eyelids grew heavier and heavier and soon he dozed off.

Max was awakened by Merlin, who was standing on the hay bale, growling a deep, low, warning growl. "What is it, Merlin?" Max whispered uneasily. He could see the hair on the back of Merlin's neck standing straight up and could feel the hair on the back of his own neck doing the same. He peered into the dim barn, trying to see what Merlin was growling at.

Max heard a latch rattle, followed by the familiar sounds of a stall door sliding open and a horse's feet clopping on the concrete floor. Max stood on his knees, alarmed, trying to see what was happening. He saw a person in the dim light, leading a horse. Then he saw something fall out of the person's pocket as the person led the horse away.

"Keith," he whispered fiercely, shaking his friend.

"What?" Keith said, instantly awake.

"Someone's taking a horse out!" Max told him.

The two boys cautiously peeked over the bales, just in time to see Quasar's hindquarters and tail heading out the door. Max and Keith grabbed each other's jacket sleeves at the same time.

"Keith!" Max screamed in a whisper.

"It's the bad guy!" Keith said urgently.

"He's taking Quasar!" Max said frantically.

"Well, what do we do?" Keith shouted in a whisper.

Max thought for a second. What would the sheriff do in the cowboy movies? "We follow him!" he said.

Max and Keith climbed over the bales as fast as they could. On the way, Max scooped up the thing that the thief had dropped. It was a glove. He shoved it deep into the pocket of his shorts as he and Keith hurried to the edge of the barn door and peered into the darkness. For a moment, they saw nothing. Then Max spotted the shape of a person and a horse moving down the path toward the woods. "There he goes,"

Max said, pointing at the thief leading Quasar away. "Come on!"

With Merlin at their heels, they ran down the path after the horse thief. Max made sure they kept a safe distance from the thief so they wouldn't be heard. Suddenly, the thief turned off the path and stopped. Max and Keith had to dive into the bushes beside the path so they wouldn't be seen. Max couldn't make out the person's face in the shadows. Whoever it was wore a dark jacket with a hood. Max couldn't even tell what color hair the person had.

The thief tied the lead rope to either side of the horse's halter, then leaped expertly onto Quasar's back. Max realized that the thief would outdistance them in no time on horseback. Then Max remembered that he still had the camera with him. He lifted it and managed to snap one picture of the thief on Quasar's back. The flash lit up the whole area for a second, and Max cringed, hoping they hadn't been seen.

At that moment the rider stopped, turned Quasar, and trotted directly toward the bushes where Max and Keith were hiding.

"Duck," Keith whispered.

Max ducked his head and held his breath, his heart pounding. He heard Quasar's hoofbeats pass right by them on the path. Max stayed in a crouch, not daring to look up. Sweat trickled down the sides of his face. He began to itch all over, but he didn't move a muscle.

Abruptly, the rider turned Quasar around again and

105

cantered off, vanishing into the dark woods beyond the path.

Max breathed a sigh of relief as he and Keith scrambled out of the bushes. "Did the picture come out?" Keith asked.

"I don't know," Max said, scratching himself furiously. He stared at the Polaroid. "I can't tell if it's developing or not, it's so dark out here." He looked up at the starlit sky, wishing the slender crescent moon were bigger and brighter. "Let's go back up to the stables and take a look at it."

They hurried back up the path, stopping at a streetlight near the entrance to the stable grounds. Max held up the snapshot. There, very plainly, was a picture of a person in a dark, hooded jacket on a large chestnut horse.

"It came out!" Keith said gleefully. "Excellent!"

"But it's the person's back. We still can't see his—or her—face," Max said with disappointment.

"So? It's still evidence. Now, if we tell the rangers or the security guys, they have something to go on." Keith said. "Come on, let's find someone."

Max thought about telling the rangers. They could go straight to the office and tell whoever was on night duty what they had seen. Then he remembered how mad Tina had been when Max had sent her after the bad guy who turned out to be an Olympic official. "Do you think they'll believe us?" he asked doubtfully.

"Max, we saw him take Quasar with our own eyes! And we have a photo to back it up. They'll have to believe us," Keith said.

Max shook his head. "No they won't. And you know what else? Tomorrow is the start of the Three-Day Event. If Quasar's not back by seven A.M., Sharon will be disqualified. It's already four o'clock," he said, checking his watch. "And we're not even supposed to be here. If we go tell the rangers right now, they're just going to yell at us for being out here. They're probably not even going to start looking for Quasar until daylight. They might not find him in time!"

"So what do we do?" Keith said impatiently.

Max said, "I have an idea. At least we know what direction the horse thief went. I bet Merlin can find him. We'll give him something of Quasar's to sniff, and he can follow the trail. They can't have gone far. We'll find out where Quasar is, *then* we'll go tell the rangers," Max said. "And," he added, "then maybe we won't get in trouble for being out here at the Horse Park all by ourselves at night."

"I see what you mean," Keith said thoughtfully. "Okay. Let's go get Merlin."

The two boys went back to the barn and found Quasar's saddle pad, which they would use to let Merlin pick up the scent. Before they went out again, Max said, "Should we wake the girls?"

"Nah," Keith said. "They'll just want to come along, and you know how noisy they are. We can handle this ourselves."

Max nodded. "Right. Come on, then." He called Merlin softly and started for the door. Then he felt Keith grab his arm and pull him back against the wall. A second later, a security guard walked by, peered into the dark barn for a few seconds, then went on his way, whistling to himself.

"Whew," Max said when he had gone. "That was a close one." Merlin came bounding up to him just then. Max caught him and clipped a leadrope to the dog's collar.

They sneaked out of the barn and scurried down the path to the spot where the thief had vanished into the woods with Quasar. "Sit, Merlin," Max told the dog.

Merlin sat down, his ears pricked forward and his tongue hanging out. He seemed to be waiting for Max to tell him the plan. Max patted him. "Good dog," he told him. "Listen, boy. Quasar's in big trouble, and we're the only ones who can help him. You've got to follow his trail and find Quasar."

Max held out Quasar's saddle pad to Merlin, who sniffed at it enthusiastically. "You smell him, boy?" Max asked. "Find him, Merlin! Find Quasar!"

Merlin barked and stood up, already starting toward the woods. "You see, Keith?" Max said excitedly. "He knows! He knows what we want."

They plunged into the dark woods, Max holding tightly to the end of the lead line as Merlin forged ahead, hot on the trail of the vanished horse. He seemed very sure of where he was taking them and only paused once to sniff the air. Max saw his wet, black nose in the pale starlight. The dog seemed to drink the cool night air, his ears folded, his eyes half closed, all his attention on the smells he was taking in with his sensitive nose. All at once he found the scent again and was off, Max holding the end of the leash for dear life as he stumbled along behind.

It was rough going. Time and again, the boys tripped over roots and rocks or felt the jarring sensation of stepping down into a hollow where they expected level ground. Soon their faces and arms were scratched by brambles. Once, Max ran right into a tree. The rough bark scraped his cheek and stung, and then smarted even more when sweat trickled into it. Max's breath came in ragged gasps, and he could hear Keith behind him sounding just the same. Max pinched himself, just to make sure he wasn't having a nightmare.

They had been going hard for ten or fifteen minutes when Merlin finally stopped at the edge of a clearing in the woods. Max could make out the shape of an old log cabin silhouetted against the sky. Merlin sat down, panting.

"This must be it," Max said breathlessly. He rested his hands on his knees. "Quasar has got to be around here somewhere."

"Do you think he's in the cabin?" Keith said.

"Maybe. We'll check it out as soon as we catch our breath."

In the darkness, they heard a horse nickering softly, the way Max had often heard Popsicle nicker when he was feeling lonely. "Did you hear that?" Max asked.

"Do you think that was Quasar?" Keith asked.

Then the horse whinnied out loud almost as if he had heard the boys talking and was calling out to them. Quasar had a funny way of whinnying that was all his own.

"That's Quasar, all right." Max smiled. "I'd recognize that whinny anywhere." He stooped to pat Merlin. "Good boy, Merlin," Max said, scratching him behind the ears. Merlin gave his gruff, low bark and stood up, looking intently into the shadows. "What's the matter, boy?" Max asked.

Suddenly, Max felt someone grab him by the hair. "Hey!" he yelled, startled. "Let go! Ow!" Keith was yelling too. Max saw that he was being held the same way.

"Shush!" a man's voice said sternly. He gave their hair an extra yank. They both quit yelling. Max tried to see the person's face, but whoever it was held them both firmly by the hair so they couldn't turn around. The man was pushing them toward the log cabin.

Max heard Merlin growl a deep, threatening growl. Then he saw a black-and-white blur as Merlin launched himself at the man who held them. He heard the man curse and felt him quicken his pace. Max stumbled and almost fell as he was pushed forward. He could hear Merlin barking and growling. Then he heard him yelp painfully, as if he had been kicked or hit hard.

"Merlin!" Max cried, before he was shoved into the dark, stuffy inside of the old log cabin. He landed hard on the wood floor, then grunted as Keith landed on top of him. The door slammed shut. There was the sound of a latch being fastened, then silence.

Max scrambled out from under Keith, wincing as

he felt pain shoot through his knee and elbow, and ran to the door. He pushed at it, first with his hands, then with his shoulder, but it didn't budge. Max backed up a few steps and ran at the door. He slammed into it with all his might but it stayed shut. Frustrated, he kicked at the door with the heel of his sneaker. "Open up!" he cried out. "Now!" Then he realized it was no use and sat down with his back against the door, rubbing his shoulder.

Max hadn't had a chance to be scared when the man had grabbed them. He had been too startled, and the hair-pulling had hurt too much. He rubbed the back of his head, remembering.

But now Max was terrified. It was very still and dark in the little cabin. He could feel thick dust under his hands where they rested on the plank floor. His heart was thumping twice as fast and loud as it ever had. He was dripping with sweat and suddenly could not remember ever being so thirsty. "Keith?" he said fearfully.

"I'm here," Keith answered.

"Are you okay?" Max asked.

"I think so," Keith said. His voice trembled. "I think we're in big trouble."

"I know," Max said.

They were silent. "What'll we do?" Keith asked. He sounded as if he was about to cry.

Max did not want to get up. His knee was hurting badly now, and his elbow felt sticky with blood where he had banged it when he fell. But with a grunt he slowly got to his feet, pushing himself up from the floor with his good arm and leg. He leaned against the door, feeling the solid boards against his back. Directly across from him, the night sky glowed faintly through the cracks of a boarded-up window. "Maybe we can get out that window somehow," he said to Keith.

"It's worth a try," Keith said.

Max made his way over to the window and tested the boards. They were nailed on tightly and wouldn't budge, however hard he pushed on them. Then he groped his way around the room, hoping to find a piece of furniture or anything he could use as a tool to try to break through the door or pry the boards off the window. But the abandoned cabin was empty. He found his way back to the door and slumped against it.

"There's no way out," he said. "I guess we wait here until somebody finds us."

But what if nobody finds us? he was thinking. He felt tears choking his throat. *What if nobody finds Quasar, either?* Then a terrible thought came to him, *What if Merlin's hurt out there somewhere?* He remembered how the dog had tried to save them and how he had yelped in pain. Max slowly drew up his knees and rested his head on his arms. Tears of frustration and fear rolled down his face, stinging his wounded cheek. *How will we ever get out of here?* he wondered.

He heard Keith crawling across the floor toward him. "Max?" Keith said tentatively.

"I'm right here, by the door," Max said. He felt Keith's hand brush his ear as he groped his way over.

Keith sat down next to Max with his back against the door.

"Looks like we really goofed," Keith said.

"No kidding," Max said.

"We should have told Megan and Chloe where we were going," Keith said forlornly. "At least then they could tell somebody where to look for us."

"They'll be looking for us as soon as it's daylight," Max said, trying to sound cheerful. Then he sighed. "Boy, are we going to be in trouble when they find us," he said with dismay. "And the worst part is, we still didn't manage to save Quasar. Poor Sharon." He shook his head sadly.

"Who do you think the thief was?" Keith asked.

Max thought back to the scene of the horse thief leading Quasar out the door. The person hadn't been very tall; Max remembered how the thief had vaulted onto the big warmblood's back almost effortlessly and cantered away with just a halter and a leadline. He was an experienced rider, whoever he was.

Then Max tried to remember the person's voice. He hadn't said anything except "Shush" when he and Keith had yelled for help. It was hard to recognize someone's voice from just one word, but Max thought it sounded a tiny bit familiar. Then he remembered that there had been a slightly sweet smell about the man who had grabbed them. Where had he smelled it before?

In a rush of recognition he knew what the smell was: teaberry gum. And he knew where he had

113

smelled it before. "Keith, I know who stole Quasar!" Max said excitedly.

"Who?" Keith asked.

"Sandy Rance," Max said. "I'm sure of it." It was starting to make sense. Max thought out loud: "Remember the story he told us about how Sharon got to ride in the Olympics instead of him? And how he lost all his money from his sponsors? Well, Amanda told me her dad sponsors Sandy. He's next on the list to ride, if anything happens to one of the main team members. Remember how he said he lost a bunch of his horses and had to pay a big lawsuit and all? I bet if he rides in the Olympics, he'll get asked to do television commercials and big companies will give him lots of money. I'll bet you anything Sandy was the one who tried to get Quasar disqualified by giving him drugs! When that didn't work, he decided to just steal him."

"Wow," Keith said. "It makes sense, doesn't it?"

"Yep," Max said. "And remember that weird gum that Sandy chews?"

"Teaberry, I remember!" Keith said. "I smelled it when he was making us walk to the cabin."

"It has to be Sandy," Max said firmly. He stood up, ignoring the pain in his knee. "We've got to tell Sharon!"

"Great idea," Keith said dejectedly, "if only we weren't locked in a log cabin somewhere in a thousand-acre park in the middle of the night."

9

Max slumped back to the floor beside Keith. They knew who the thief was. They knew where Quasar was. But they could do nothing to stop Sharon from being disqualified from riding in the Olympics. Max was completely frustrated.

He noticed that the dim room was a tiny bit brighter, and the light that seeped in between the cracks in the boards was the blue-gray color of early dawn. Keith's face appeared as a lighter blob in the gloom of the cabin. Max could just barely make out the face of his watch, but he couldn't see the hands. The equestrian games were supposed to start at eight o'clock. He felt a tiny bit hopeful. Maybe as the room grew brighter, they would be able to see some way to get out.

Suddenly, Max heard a scratching sound. "Listen," he whispered. "Did you hear that?"

"Is it a rat?" Keith asked fearfully. "I don't like rats."

"I hope not," Max said. They listened and heard the sound again. "It's on the other side of the door," Max said. He tried to peer through one of the cracks, but it was still too dark to see much. The scratching went on, faster and more purposeful. Then Max heard a bark. "Merlin!" he said. "Keith, it's Merlin! Maybe he can get us out somehow!"

"Max?" someone said quietly from outside the door.

"Megan? Is that you?" Max said in disbelief.

"Yes," she said. "Hang on, we're trying to get the door open."

"Hurry!" Max urged.

In another moment, there was a scraping sound and the door swung open with a jerk. Max and Keith had been crowded up against it. They both fell out the door when it opened, landing on the ground in a heap, right on top of Megan and Chloe. Merlin ran around in happy circles, stopping every few seconds to lick frantically at Max's face.

"Do you mind getting off me?" Megan said. The kids untangled themselves and got to their feet. Max grabbed his sister and hugged her.

"I've never been so happy to see you in all my life!" Max exclaimed.

"And you probably never will be again," Megan joked.

"How did you find us?" Keith asked.

Megan and Chloe smiled at each other. " 'Let's not wake up Megan and Chloe. Girls make too much noise,' " Megan said, imitating Max's words. "I'll bet you're glad we woke up anyway."

"We sure are," Max said gratefully.

"We'll never leave you out again," Keith promised.

"But how *did* you find us?" Max asked.

"We followed you when you came back to the barn to get Quasar's saddle pad," Chloe said.

"Then we lost you in the woods, but Merlin found us and led us back here," Megan explained.

Max bent to hug the dog, who squirmed joyfully. "What a good dog you are, Merlin," he said. And he meant it with all his heart.

The sky had begun to turn pink, and the colors of the trees and grasses were starting to emerge from the gray gloom. They searched the area all around the cabin, but there was no sign of Quasar. "Let's get back to the barn, fast," Max said. "We have to tell the rangers what happened to Quasar. They'll be able to find him."

"Does anyone know the way back?" Keith asked.

Max thought he knew which direction they needed to go. He recalled seeing the sun setting over the woods when he had ridden with Tina. That meant the rising sun was in the direction of the stables. In the growing light the four children hurried through the woods and managed to find their way back to the road. On the way, Max and Keith told Megan and Chloe about Sandy.

At last they reached the main barn and ran to find the rangers. But when they got to the office they found it empty. A few grooms were around, beginning to feed and water the horses. "Where are the rangers?" Max asked one of the grooms, who was leading Gypsy Rose into her stall.

"Barn two," he said, pointing.

The children hurried to the barn and found Sharon talking to Tina and another park ranger. Several security guards were walking around. They looked suspiciously at Max and the other kids when they pounded into the barn. "Sharon!" Max yelled.

"Max! What are you—" She stopped, looking startled at first, then alarmed. "What on earth happened to you?" She ran to his side.

"Max, are you okay?" Tina said with concern.

Max remembered that he must look terrible after the long night of running through the woods. He glanced at his elbow and saw a messy scrape, smeared with dirt and still oozing blood. It had hurt a lot, but he shrugged it off.

"Never mind," he said impatiently. "Sharon, we know who stole Quasar!"

"What?" Sharon said. "How do you know? Who?"

The security guards gathered around as Max explained what they had seen the night before and how they had been locked in the cabin by the thief. One of the guards wrote down everything in a notebook. "And we know who the thief is—it's Sandy. Sandy Rance," Max told them. "We're sure of it!"

The guards shook their heads. Some of them even laughed. The one with the notebook closed it with a snap.

"Now, what kind of thanks is that, Max-a-million? Haven't I been a good friend to you?"

With a gasp, Max looked up and realized that Sandy was in the barn, too. He was slouched against a tack trunk nearby. He was not wearing a dark hooded jacket, but he had probably changed clothes, Max figured. Max said angrily to him, "We know it was you! Keith and I recognized your voice when you were locking us up! We saw you, and we even have a picture of you riding away on Quasar!"

Sandy looked amused. He shook his head with a sad smile. "Max-a-million, I thought you and I were friends."

"Let's see the picture," Tina said.

Max showed them the Polaroid. The adults were all silent. "Max," Tina said, "this is a picture of a person's back. You can't tell who it is. You can't even tell if it's a man or a woman."

"You see, boys?" Sandy said. "You can't just blame somebody for a crime. You got to have some real, hard evidence. Besides, why would I steal my own teammate's horse? That wouldn't be very sporting of me, would it?"

Max turned to Sharon again. "Sharon, listen. Sandy told us how he was eliminated from riding at the last Olympic Games because Quasar was lame. He told us about almost losing his business and having to sell off his horses. He's just trying to get even with you because you rode in his place, and now you have Quasar. And, Amanda told me her dad sponsors Sandy. He'll make a ton of money if he rides. Sandy

119

was the one who tried to drug Quasar—I know it—
just so he could ride on the Three-Day team instead
of you. And somebody walked in before he could finish the job. So then he came back and stole Quasar."

"Well, now," Sandy said. "You sure are a smart one,
aren't you, boy? You have a pretty good theory there,
but there's just one little hole in it."

Sharon said, "Max, Quasar's not the only horse that
was stolen."

"What do you mean?" Max said.

"Marauder's gone, too," Sharon said.

Max's mouth dropped open. Then he closed it
again. He felt his ears grow hot, as the flush of em-
barrassment spread over his face and all the way to
his toes. He didn't know what to say.

Sandy began to laugh. "You see there, Max-a-million?
I couldn't steal my own horse, now, could I?"

"Be quiet, Sandy," Sharon said. "He feels bad
enough." She turned to Max. "I want you to come
with me. I'm going to call your dad and tell him
you're okay. He'll be very worried if he wakes up and
finds you all missing."

The kids followed the adults back to the main barn.
Tina and the other ranger began to tack their horses.
Most of the mounted officers had already been sent
out to search for the missing horses. Sharon used the
phone in the rangers' office to call James Morrison.

"Your dad's on his way," she told Max when she
came out. "Stay right here," Sharon said to the children. She and Sandy began talking to the security

120

guards nearby. Max, Keith, Megan, and Chloe sat down on a trunk across from Gypsy's stall.

"I thought for sure it was Sandy," Max said dejectedly. "I can't understand how his horse could be gone, too."

Keith pointed to the empty stall next to them. The sign on the stall wall said MARAUDER. The stall guard hung down, unfastened. The stall was empty.

"Maybe he just got scared that we knew too much, and so he took Marauder out too," Megan whispered, eyeing Sandy, a few yards away. "That way he would look innocent."

"How could he have had time to hide her, too? It was getting to be light soon after we got into the cabin. Daylight is feeding time. He would be pretty stupid to try and steal his own horse when the grooms would be up and around," Max said. He glanced at his watch. "Six twenty-five," he said. "The check-in deadline is seven o'clock. I hope they find Quasar before it's too late."

"I hope they find one of the horses, at least," Sharon said. "Margaux Weinstock's horse, Outlander, came up lame yesterday. She was the other alternate rider. That means that unless they find one or both of our horses, the Three-Day team will have to compete with only three riders. All the other teams will have four riders. The United States won't be able to win a medal with such a low team score."

It was like Sharon, Max thought, to be more worried about the team than about herself or her own horse. Max was watching Gypsy Rose as he listened to Sharon. The mare stuck her flea-bitten head out over her stall guard and began to nibble at the clip that fastened it. Suddenly, it came undone.

"Look, you guys," Max said curiously as Gypsy stepped out of her stall. "Gypsy just got out."

Sharon and Sandy turned to watch with amusement as Gypsy walked over to another stall and undid the latch with her nimble lips! The door swung open as the horse, a bay gelding, walked out of his stall and followed Gypsy down the barn aisle. The kids and adults watched, astonished. Then everybody laughed, including the security guards.

"Looks like we found our thief, doesn't it, kiddies?" Sandy said. "I'll bet she let the horses out in the night. They're probably wandering around the park, eating grass. I betcha the rangers will find them in no time."

Megan led the big bay horse back into his stall, while Max caught Gypsy. He put her into her stall and clipped the stall guard.

"She does that all the time," one of the grooms said. "But she's never let out another horse before. Usually, she just wanders around the barn until I come in and put her back into her stall. I guess she ought to have a special latch on her stall door."

Max was staring at Gypsy's stall guard. Something was bothering him—a little teasing thought hidden deep in his brain, one that he couldn't quite bring to the surface. *Something about the latches on the stalls* . . . He frowned, trying to remember. Then he had it. "Sharon!" he yelled.

Sharon jumped. "Max, please don't yell like that.

This is a barn. And you scared me half to death," she added.

"The latches!" Max was pointing. "All of the stalls in this barn have the same doors. They have these latches, and the doors swing open and closed. In the new barns, the doors *slide* open or closed. And they have different latches. Gypsy might have let Marauder out, since she was in this barn, but there's no way she could have let Quasar out! A human had to do it—the doors are horse-proof!"

Sandy took a pack of gum out of his pocket. "Well, now, that's one smart little Arabian," Sandy said, unwrapping a stick of gum. "I'll betcha Gypsy Rose could undo any latch she set her mind to." He put the gum in his mouth and chewed it thoughtfully.

"Excuse me, Sandy, you dropped this," Chloe said. She picked up a brown leather riding glove from the floor and handed it politely to Sandy. "It fell out of your pocket when you took out the gum."

"Thank you, Sugar," Sandy said, showing Chloe his most charming gap-toothed grin. He felt in his pocket. "Now, where's my other one? Don't tell me I dropped it, too . . ." He patted his pockets, searching for the other glove.

Max stared at Sandy. He reached into the pocket of his shorts and pulled out the glove that the thief had dropped the night before. Slowly, Max began to smile. "Oh, Sandy," he said casually. "Which glove are you missing?"

"The left one," Sandy said.

Max held out the glove, a left-hand, brown leather

riding glove. "The thief dropped this glove last night, on his way out of the barn," Max said. As he held up the glove, a scrap of paper fluttered out of it. Max bent to pick it up. It was a pink wrapper from a stick of teaberry gum. "And the thief was chewing teaberry gum," Max said. "He was chewing it when he threw us in the cabin—Keith and I smelled it!"

The security guards looked at Sandy, who coughed. He had swallowed his gum. "Let's see your glove, son," one of the guards said to Sandy. Sandy handed his glove to the guard, who compared it with the one Max had found. "Looks like we got us a match here," the guard said. He stepped toward Sandy. "That makes you our number one suspect for horse stealing," he said.

Sandy's eyes looked everywhere but at the guard. His face was turning redder by the second. Suddenly, he turned and bolted out of the barn, before anyone could stop him.

Tina had just led Mounty outside.

"Tina!" Max yelled. "He's getting away!"

Tina swung into the saddle and galloped after Sandy. The kids watched from the door as she chased him down and ordered him to stop. Finally he stopped running. She dismounted, took the silver handcuffs from her belt, and slapped them around his wrists behind his back. They all cheered when she marched him back up to the barn.

Sandy was sneering. "So you think it's me. You'll never prove it." His face was set in hard lines as he glared at Sharon, then Tina. "They tried to say I killed those two horses for the insurance money, too, but they couldn't prove that, either. That's the beauty of the justice system. You're innocent until proven guilty."

"We'll prove it this time, Sandy," Sharon said. "Just you wait."

"Well, you still don't have your horse, do you, Sharon?" Sandy said. "Looks like you won't be riding in this Olympics," he said over his shoulder as the guards led him away.

Sharon stood glaring after Sandy until he was out of sight. But then Max saw her shoulders droop sadly. "I guess he's right about that," she said softly, unbuttoning the shiny gold buttons on her fancy black shadbelly coat. "If I don't have a horse at the check-in in twenty minutes, I don't ride." She took off her elegant black top hat and smoothed the perfect bun underneath it.

Max thought he saw the gleam of tears in Sharon's eyes. He stared at his trainer, dressed in her *grand prix* dressage outfit, with no horse to compete on, and he wished he could do something to help. Suddenly he had an idea.

Max glanced at his watch. Pulling Tina away from the group, he quickly told her what he was thinking. Tina nodded in agreement.

"Merlin," Max called, and he whistled. The dog came running up to him. "Merlin, find Quasar," Max said. "Find him!"

Merlin barked in reply and ran out the barn door. The kids and Sharon watched him streak down the path and disappear into the woods, with Tina and Mounty cantering behind.

"Do you think he can find him?" Sharon asked.

"I know he can," Max said with determination. "He did it last night. He can do it again. You just watch."

They eyed the trees anxiously. After five, then ten minutes, there was still no sign of the dog. Max and Megan exchanged worried glances. No one spoke.

Finally Sharon checked her own watch. "I'm afraid there's just not enough time," she said sadly. She turned and started for the barn, shaking her head.

"Sharon, look!" Max shouted. "Here they come!" He pointed excitedly to the path. Merlin was herding two horses, a black and a chestnut. Tina was cantering along behind.

Sharon spun around to look. Max saw both her eyebrows go shooting up on her forehead. "Is it Quasar?" she asked in disbelief. "It *is* Quasar!"

"It's him, it's him!" Megan shouted, jumping up and down. She and Chloe hugged each other.

"There's still time before the check-in!" Max shouted, as Quasar and Marauder trotted eagerly to their stalls. Sharon caught Quasar and quickly led him away toward the inspection panel. A groom followed along, brushing him as they went.

Tina got off Mounty. She was holding a bucket and a lead line. "That dog went straight to the horses. Quasar was tied to a tree with this lead line. There was a bucket of water nearby. I guess Sandy just planned to keep him tied up long enough to disqualify him. I don't think he counted on Gypsy letting his

126

horse loose. She was standing near where Merlin found Quasar. That's one smart dog," Tina said with admiration.

"He sure is," Max said, hugging Merlin. "He wasn't supposed to come to the Olympics, but I don't know what we would have done without him."

A few days after the equestrian games were over, Max and Megan and Keith and Chloe sat on Max's tack trunk at Thistle Ridge Farm, talking about their Olympic adventure.

"Wasn't it great how Sharon and Quasar ended up winning the gold medal in the Three-Day Event?" Megan said.

"If she hadn't ridden, the United States team couldn't have won the team gold medal," Keith said.

"Wasn't it great that we actually helped the United States Equestrian team by helping to find Quasar?" Chloe said.

"Boy, were we glad to see you and Chloe when we were locked up in that cabin," Max told Megan.

"Yeah, we'll never try to leave you girls out of anything again," Keith said.

"Hey, we never did think of a motto for the Short Stirrup Club," Megan said.

"We don't need a motto," Max said. "We just need teamwork!"

A black-and-white blur came racing down the barn aisle and jumped right into Max's lap. "And Merlin!" he added. "I guess we'd better make him an honorary member of the Short Stirrup Club," Max said.

The dog barked happily, and they all laughed. Max stuck out his hand, and the other kids piled their hands on top. Merlin watched curiously, then put a paw on top of the hands. As they cheered for the Short Stirrup Club, Max wondered what their *next* adventure would be!

About the Author

ALLISON ESTES grew up in Oxford, Mississippi. She wrote, bound, and illustrated her first book when she was five years old, learned to drive her grandfather's truck when she was eight, and got her first pony when she was ten. She has been writing, driving trucks, and riding horses ever since.

Allison is a trainer at Claremont Riding Academy, the only riding stable in New York City. She currently lives in Manhattan with her seven-year-old daughter, Megan, who spends every spare moment around, under, or on horses.

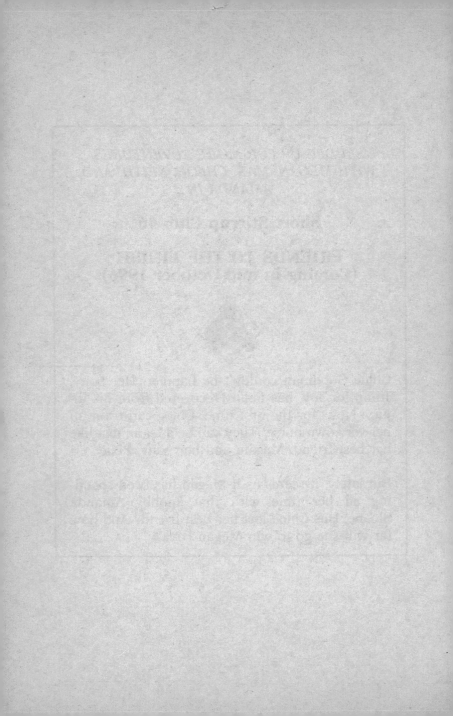